The Lama Drama

Janet Philp

Published by Anatomy Fundamentals

First published by Anatomy Fundamentals 2019
47 Liberton Gardens, Edinburgh EH16 6JT

ISBN 978-0-9955101-4-2

Published by Anatomy Fundamentals

This book is dedicated to everyone who has wondered what lies beyond.

An answer to your existential dread is within.

1

The security camera slowly panned through the gloom that was the underground car park. It reached the end of its arc and, with a mechanical groan, started its return journey.

"37 seconds." Martin slid down the side of the car that he had braced himself against and looked at his watch again. It was his favourite watch; Mickey's big hand pointed to the six, his small hand to the ten and his tail had just appeared from behind his right ear. 37 seconds. What could he do in 37 seconds? If he had remembered to bring the spray paint he could probably have blacked out the camera lens. He conducted a quick search of his jacket pockets. He was armed with two, two pence pieces, half a packet of sugar free gum and 8 inches of a ruler. It had been 12 inches long but that had left an annoying four inches sticking out of his inside pocket.

There was no choice; he would have to break in.

Breaking into a car in under 30 seconds would be child's play to your average street corner hoodlum but it had been years since Martin's last attempt and car security had progressed. He slid back down the side of the car with six inches of plastic ruler as Mickey's tail disappeared behind his ear. He sat and stared at the mangled end of his ruler for the next two camera sweeps.

"It's never like this in the movies." He glanced at his watch again as he prepared himself for another futile attempt. Futile because even he knew that a six inch ruler was not long enough.

"If you don't open this time I'll just put my foot through the window." He patted the door panel and slid the ruler into place, it disappeared without a sound.

"Give me a break!" He muttered under his breath.

Engineers have worked on vehicle security since the wheel was invented. There have been steering locks to ensure you drive around in circles. Alarms that will wake the dead at fifty yards, disablers to ensure the engine does not start, automatic engine disarming devices, the list is endless. And yet they have never developed anything that protects a car from a direct threat of violence and the power of prayer. As Martin's ruler disappeared between the window and the seal, he tried the handle and the door gave way below his hand and swung open. He slid into the driving seat with a little smirk on his face. The thought that the car door might have been open all along was pushed to the back of his mind. The nudge from the muzzle of the gun below his ear caused the smirk to drop.

"And what the hell do you think you are doing?" The grunt came from behind, advertising that its owner maybe wasn't the brightest thing on the planet.

"Valet service?"

The gun smacked into the back of his head with a sickening crash and Martin fell forward, face first, onto the hand brake.

One of the problems with being dead, and let's face it there are quite a few, is that you don't bleed anymore. Whilst this obviously has its good points, it is not much of a comfort when you are being beaten senseless by a mindless thug. The sort of individual who is seeking the satisfaction of a spurt of blood or a large bruise appearing.

"Are you ready to talk yet?" The brains of the operation swung his legs down from the desk and sauntered over. There were in a small office dimly lit from one large overhead light. It looked like the set from a 1970's television series; almost as if someone had tried to set up a typical gangster hide out.

"I've told you, I was trying to nick the car." Martin gave his beaten head a shake to try and clear his senses.

"I don't believe you." The thin suited man placed one foot on the chair that Martin was tied to and peered down into his face. He was a little disappointed at the lack of colour and swelling.

"Why not? It's a nice car."

The man gave a snort. He pulled a packet of cigarettes out of his jacket pocket and slipped one into his mouth. He started to talk, the cigarette jumping around widely.

"This car park is miles out of town, it's not signposted and it's full of 'nice' cars. You want me to believe you are an opportunistic car thief." He paused to light the cigarette, took a deep breath and blew the smoke into Martin's face. Even that amount of smoke did not hide the rancid smell of his breath. "Now, tell me who you are working for or I'll get Eric here to give you a little more beating."

Martin had discovered over the years that, if all else fails, the truth is usually a pretty safe bet. In his case, the truth was usually more unlikely than any fabrication he could come up with.

"Ok, ok." He tried to look despondent as he volunteered the information. "I work for a large organisation."

"Trying to steal our slice of the pie?" The man returned to his stance of crouching over Martin.

"Trying to stop you eating it."

"I knew it, I knew it." The man slammed his fist into his other open palm and gave a little grin to Eric. "Are you West Coast based?"

"In a manner of speaking." As Martin spoke the man kicked the base of his seat so that Martin tumbled backwards onto the floor, still tied to the chair. His head thumped into the floor with a sickening crash.

"I knew it." The man seemed to give a little jump for joy. "Kill him Eric."

"Hang on, hang on - I told you what you wanted to know." Martin squirmed on the floor like a fish out of water.

"I know, and now you are no use to me." He nodded to Eric who produced his automatic pistol and pointed it slowly at Martin's forehead. Even Eric wasn't going to miss from this range. He started to squeeze back the trigger.

"Wait, Wait." His boss dived into his jacket pocket and produced a small mobile phone which had just started to ring. "I don't want too much background noise." He smiled a sickly grin at Martin and turned to the handset. "Hello, Brian Trumpton here." There was a blinding flash and then everything was quiet. Very quiet indeed.

2

"Here." The young lady slid the car keys across the reception desk. She was dressed in jeans and a sweat shirt and appeared far too confident for her own good. "And you can have this too."

"And this is, madam?" The even younger lady behind the reception desk reached across and took the pile of paperwork.

"It's a bill that I don't intend to settle."

"Is that because it has already been settled madam?" The final word was becoming more and more insulting.

"No, it's because the car was under warranty."

"It states at the top of the page that warranty expired on the 27th of last month and this work was conducted on the 3rd of this month."

"Yes," Jayne tried to match the patronising tone of the receptionist but she hadn't had the years of practice. "But, the work that was performed on the 3rd was replacing something that your mechanics broke on the 25th."

The receptionist stared at her for a minute, expressionless.

"I'll have to clear this with the manager." She turned to walk off.

"Hang on." Jayne called out after her and she turned back with a triumphant smirk; people didn't usually push on the warrant date issue. "Clear it with the manager later - we can continue this when I pick up my car this afternoon. I can't afford to wait any longer; I'm late as it is. So, if you'll just give me the keys to the courtesy car."

"Late for what?" The receptionist burnt her remaining bridge by looking Jayne up and down with a very critical eye.

"Late for the embalming of my uncle Hector." Jayne lied.

"Oh, I'm so sorry madam, courtesy car did you say." The receptionist face, now the same colour as her vile red nail varnish, flicked through the file on the desk. "Just a moment." She reached over to the intercom mouth piece. "Brian to reception, Brian to reception." She smiled sweetly across to Jayne. "He won't be a moment."

She spoke the truth because a second later a spotty youth burst through the door and the reception area was momentarily bathed in loud music.

"Brian, this lady has brought her car in for a service and the courtesy car appears to be booked out." The receptionists tried to mutter under her breath, not the easiest thing to do whilst chewing gum.

"Oh, that's alright." Brian reached across the desk and thumbed through the file leaving large black fingerprints on each page. He got to the page in question and tapped it several times. "Mr Johnston. He was booked in for a service but he's called off." He patted his overall pockets and produced a set of keys. "It's around the back, the Escort with the red door. Watch the wipers though, they don't work very well if they get too wet." Jayne took the keys and picked up her bag.

"See you later Madam." The receptionist called after her, "and I do hope your uncle is feeling better."

If Jayne had been paying a bit more attention then she would have been suspicious of the description of the car as 'the one with the red door' but it fitted exactly. The rest of the car was jet black, the driver's door was red lead.

"Oh, Great." She dropped her bag as she attempted to open the door, it stuck. The passenger's door was more forgiving and after a few well aimed thumps, it sprung open. Jayne threw her bag into the back, beside spanners and a selection of magazines that she didn't wish to examine too closely, and slid across to the driver's seat. The keys slipped into the ignition, although with the number of wires hanging down below the dashboard, Jayne wondered if keys were really a necessity. At least the engine worked. She glanced at her watch. There was no danger of her being late. She was meeting Julia, an old school friend who had never been on time in her life. Just as well really because Jayne was going to have to park around the corner and walk to the health club; they would never allow a vehicle like this into their car park. She pulled away with a stutter and crawled up the side of the garage towards the road. Jayne hated driving other people's cars. Nothing was ever in the right place. The seat was always slightly wrong, the mirrors weren't exactly right and the fluffy dice defiantly were not her. In fact, there was only one thing Jayne hated more than driving somebody else's car and that was driving somebody else's car around the North circular.

The North circular is a funny road, not that the commuters who spent hours on it every day ever found anything to laugh about. The road that courses across the north of London is the sort of thoroughfare where prior knowledge makes so much difference. Lanes come and go, filter lights take lines of traffic away and some of the junctions are horrendous. It can take anything from an hour to two and a half to traverse the capital depending on whether you managed to catch the green light wave. Jayne had not.

She pulled up to the first set of red lights. The radio was tuned into some radio station that she didn't recognise. Rather than trying to retune a strange radio she flicked through some of the preprogramed buttons and resorted to the original choice but at a lower volume.

The lights changed and the first few cars made it across the junction. Jayne pulled forwards. She would get across at the next change.

She wondered what Julia hand in mind for bridesmaid dresses now. Originally, she had produced pictures of some peach taffeta things that you wouldn't have been seen dead in aged nine, let alone now.

The lights changed again and Jayne made it across the junction and joined the next queue of traffic.

After the taffeta things, Julia had changed her mind and decided to go with a twenties style dress with a beaded cap.

The lights changes again and Jayne moved forwards to the front of the queue.

After the twenties dresses Julia had decided not to have any bridesmaids. Jayne was fairly sure there had been a faint air of relief at the lunch when Julia had made that announcement. None of the University friends were really looking forward to dressing up. Jayne had been given the role of maid of honour but in actual fact she was the only unmarried one of the group. She pulled a packet of mints out of her jeans pocket and popped one of them into her mouth.

The lights changed again and Jayne crossed the junction into the next queue.

Of course, she was further away from being married now than ever before. Not that she had ever been close to it but she had eventually mustered up the courage to give Edward the heave ho last month. Ditching your boyfriend a month before the biggest wedding in your social group was a sure sign of madness according to Julia, but Jayne had had enough of the mundane existence that had become her life.

The lights changed and Jayne moved forward. She had received a phone call from Julia a few nights ago. She needed to see her. Jayne wondered what on Earth it could be about. It was probably about the latest bridesmaid plan but it could be about Edward. She wasn't sure. Julia had been quite concerned about the seating plan. How could Jayne have split up with Edward when she knew the effect it would have on the reception.

The lights changed again. Jayne was two cars from the front.

Oh well she would just have to wait and see. Jayne glanced at her watch. She could make it in time. The lights had just gone amber, Jayne dithered for a moment and then put her foot down.

She thought she was going to get away with it right up until the moment the headlights blazed in her side windows and the whole car shook.

3

Side impact bars hadn't been invented when the courtesy car had been made. The nose of the tank like Volvo was taking up most of the interior of Jayne's car, its lights still blazing, its engine still running. There were noises all around, horns, voices, people shouting and then, in the distance, just as her eyes were starting to close and the edges of her vision were going blurry, she heard the ambulance siren.

"Well, hello there." Jayne woke to find a middle aged man studying her face with a pen light. He smiled warmly. He flicked the light into her pupil and then flicked it out to the side. He repeated the process on the other side.

"My name is Patrick. You're in a bit of a mess love. Let's see if we can make you more comfortable." He turned the light off and popped it back into the breast pocket of his dayglo jacket. "I think we had best take you with us."

"The others?" Jayne feebly tried to point towards the other car.

"They're fine. Don't you go worrying about them." He ran his hands around her face and back through her hair. "I'm just going to check the rest of you." He ran his hands over her shoulders and down her arms. She could feel the pressure as he checked for what lay under her skin. "You're lucky it came in from the side." He nodded towards the front of the Volvo that was still occupying the passenger seat of the car. "I think we ought to be able to get you out without waiting for the cutting crew. Do you feel ok?"   It seemed like a strange question but as Jayne thought about it she realised that actually she didn't feel too bad. Nothing was particularly hurting? Surely something should hurt? Maybe they already had her dosed up on painkillers, or maybe it was the adrenaline. Jayne tried to look around but she had some sort of support around her neck. She shouldn't have tried to get across those lights. "Speak to me, don't move your head."

"I'm fine." Jayne mumbled.

"I think we both know that's not true." Patrick gave a big smile. "Now let's see if we can get this seat belt off of you. I'm just going to reach across and see if we can undo it." The ambulance man reached across her lap and Jayne was surprised to hear the click as it released and momentarily wondered how he had managed to open the driver's door. Had he had to thump it or had the collision fixed it? He slowly fed the belt back across her body. Jayne was aware of a movement outside and another dayglo clad person appeared.

"I think we can get her out without the fire crew." Patrick told his colleague. "Would you like us to get you out?" Jayne was going to try and nod and then remembered the earlier advice.

"Yes please, get me out."

"Ok, we're just going to ease you forward and get this board down behind you." Jayne felt something being slipped down the back of the seat and then a Velcro band was fixed across her forehead.

"We are going to spin you around and then lift you onto the trolley. If you feel anything you don't like, you just let us know." Patrick's face popped up in front of her face, "it's going to be fine. We will get you out of here and into the ambulance." Jayne hadn't really appreciated she was moving until Patrick's face moved and she was no longer looking through the shattered windscreen.

On the count of three, she was lifted up and out of the car and placed on the trolley. She had expected it to hurt more. She could see her leg had been splinted and the bandages that had been applied were already soaked in blood, and yet she couldn't feel it. 'Oh my God, I've broken my back!' Was her first thought but surely they wouldn't have moved her if that were the case. They passed a trolley going the other way.

"Get that girl out of the escort." She heard a voice behind them shout as her rescuers slid the trolley into the back of their waiting ambulance. Girl in an escort? Had she managed to involve another car as well? How many people had she maimed in her hurry to get across the lights? The ambulance door shut behind them and they pulled away.

It was a very smooth ride. As they drove away the crew began their work. A mask was slid over her face, a drip was set up into a needle that was slid into her arm so painlessly she didn't even notice and one of them started to tend to her leg. She tried to say something.

"No, no, just you lie still. It will take you a few minutes to adjust." The smiling face appeared above her again and held the mask in place as he started to remove the neck brace and the Velcro strap over her forehead.

"Mm mn mn m?"

"Pardon me?" He lifted the edge of the mask up.

"Have I broken my leg?"

"Well now, I'm no doctor but I think the answer to that one would have to be yes and no." He smiled again as though that would explain it all.

"What?"

"Well, you have and you haven't. Now are you feeling strong enough for me to be asking you a few questions." The Irish ambulance man gave another smile. Well Jayne supposed it could make sense, there were two bones in your leg. She nodded her consent. She felt surprisingly well for having just been in a car accident.

"Name?"

"Jayne, Jayne Pottage, with a y."

"Now where would I be putting a y in Pottage?" He shot her a cheeky grin. "Now, would that be a Miss or a Mrs, and don't say Ms as I don't have a box for that."

"Miss."

"Address?"

"Flat 2b Suncrest Road."

"Did you work? What did you do?"

"I wasn't at work today. I was meant to be meeting a friend. She will be waiting..."

"I'm sure someone will let her know." Patrick gave her a reassuring smile. "This sort of news always gets to those who need to know." He patted her hand. "What did you do for a living?"

Human resource development officer." Jayne realised that was what he had meant all along.

He paused and looked down his sheet, obviously trying to decide which box that came under.

"That would be the same as personal wouldn't it, Old form you see." He ticked a box and continued. "Date of birth?"

"22nd of May 1990."

"Date of death." He glanced at his watch "15th June 2018."

"Pardon?" Jayne pulled the mask from her face.

"Date of death." He repeated. "Dear me, did you not realise that you are dead."

"I can't be dead, I'm talking to you."

"Well that's alright; I'm dead too." He gave a big grin and signed the bottom of the form. "I'll just give you this form, it should speed things up on the way through check in." Jayne lay on the bed dumbstruck, the piece of paper sitting on top of her chest.

"My leg?"

"Well, yes." He started to busy himself tidying up. "Now the leg on your body is broken, along with most of the other bits, but your spiritual leg is fine." He pulled back the blanket to show her. He was correct, her whole body appeared fine.

"So that is why it didn't hurt then."

"Oh, I suspect you went out like a light. An impact like that; no chance of surviving." He picked up the soiled bandages and stuffed them into a clinical waste bag.

"Where are we going now?"

"Well, we are going home for tea. You caught us just on our way back to the depot, but we can drop you off at the SSC."

"SSC?"

"Soul Sorting Centre. Sounds more like a fish market if you ask me. I don't know why they needed to change the name. Limbo sounded nice, don't you think?" He didn't wait for a reply. "There will be more forms to fill in and if I were you I'd have thought of a religion by then."

Jayne lay back on the bed. So, that was it then. She was dead. She stared up at the roof of the ambulance. Nothing had changed – she couldn't be dead. Any moment now she would wake up and this would all be a dream.

She couldn't actually be dead. Could she?

4

Martin stood under the shower and let the water wash all over his bruised and battered body. That had been too close that time; he had cut it fine before but not that fine. He looked up towards the shower and took a mouthful of water.

"Martin?" The shout came from the living room of his apartment.

"In here." He replied, turned the water off and reached for a towel.

"You got back then." His friend came in and sat down on the closed toilet. He was about the same age as Martin, late twenties, although his hair had started to turn grey around the temples. He was dressed casually but looked business like and harassed.

Martin stepped out the shower, wrapped the towel around his hips and walked out. "You could have come a bit earlier."

"I was waiting to see if you needed help." His friend, Simon, set off towards the small kitchen alcove and started to make coffee. Martin, who by now had located his underwear which was strewn around the room, came up to the breakfast bar and leant over it.

"I was tied to a bloody chair. What exactly did you think I was going to do?"

"I don't know." Simon calmly replied, he had been on the end of Martin's raised voice before, " but it seemed like a bloody stupid situation to get yourself into if you didn't have a plan." He smiled smugly, almost challenging Martin to come back with a reply.

"One day Simon, I am going to get you trapped down on Earth with me, see how you like it." He pulled on a shirt that had been lying across the back of the sofa.

"I don't know what you're complaining about anyway. You're dead already." He pressed the button on the coffee machine and the room was filled with the aroma.

"Yes." Martin hopped back into view, halfway through pulling his jeans on, "but I still have the back of my head. Have you seen how long those boys down in reconstruction take? I would have been out of action for ages."

"You might be anyway." Simon pushed a full mug across the counter. "We have a meeting this afternoon with the boss."

"About?"

"I'm not sure, but he didn't sound happy." Simon took his mug over to the windows.

The flat looked down into a Central Park as did all the flats in this area of town. It was a nice sunny day, just enough breeze to keep you cool but not too much. There were people out sunbathing, walking, playing, meeting people. What he wouldn't give to have an afternoon off but no, he had got a meeting with the boss from Hell, figuratively speaking of course. Why did he have to be responsible for Martin? Oh yeah sure, they got some fantastic results but always by the skin of their teeth. They succeed where others failed because they waded too far in. He took a mouthful of coffee and glanced over at his friend who was lounging on the sofa fiddling with the remote control. "I can't wait until we get Doug back as our supervisor."

Martin shot him a glance. Was it angry? Was it hopeful? Even after all these years Simon wasn't sure.

"Is that likely?" The tone gave nothing away.

"He has been back at work now for 3 months." Simon turned and lent against the window. He tried to look casual, like he hadn't been planning this conversation for weeks. "Have you been in touch?"

Martin shot him another glance, this one a little longer, as though he was trying to work out where this was going.

"Simon, we both know I haven't been in touch with him. He knows where I am, if he wants to talk to me then he can get in touch easy enough."

"It's not that easy." Simon left the window and walked around to take a seat on the sofa. "He's embarrassed. He doesn't know how to approach you. You need to do something or we are never going to get him back."

"Joshua isn't that bad as a boss, we could do a lot worse." Martin climbed in to the corner of the sofa and stretched his legs out along the seat. He pointed the remote at the television, attempting to draw the conversation to a close,

"He's not Doug! You can't throw away centuries of friendship over some stupid spat." Simon let out a sigh. That was not how he had envisaged the conversation going. Frustration had got the better of him. He wanted their old boss back but this quarrel with Martin seemed to be an obstacle. He needed to remove it. He wanted to return to the 'good old days'.

Martin was quiet for a moment. He slowly lifted his legs down and stood up.

"I have not thrown the friendship away." He paused as though searching for the words to express his thoughts. "I ignored the 'spat'." He put the word into inverted commas with his hands. "It wasn't me that took a posting miles away. You seem to be conveniently forgetting that I risked my life."

"Our lives." Simon corrected.

"I risked our lives." Martin continued, "to go and get him back from Hell. Have I seen him since then? No. Has he come to see me? No."

"He was locked up in the hospital for 6 months! How was he meant to come and see you? Did you go and see him?" It was the same argument that Martin had presented before. It is hard for the other person to make the first move when they are incarcerated.

"Simon." Martin put up his hand whilst he looked at the floor, choosing his words with care. "I want Doug back. I want the old Doug back. He did some sick things down in Hell."

"He was tricked, that wasn't him. Come on, you know Doug."

"I did know Doug." Martin realised what he had said, "I do know Doug." He corrected himself. "I've read the report. I know exactly what happened. I understand the embarrassment." Martin looked across at Simon and rubbed his hand across his lower jaw. "I..." There was a slight quiver in his voice. Simon heard it. This was a side of Martin he hadn't seen. Where was the crass over confident ex soldier? Martin pinned him to the sofa with a glare. "I don't know what to do." Martin ran his hand back through his hair and threw the remote onto the seat. "I don't know what to do." He quietly muttered as though the realisation had just dawned on him? He turned and retreated to the bedroom leaving Simon sitting on the sofa, dumbstruck

5

The portly gentleman flicked out the watch that lived in his waistcoat pocket. It was a gold affair complete with chain and although some people claimed it made him look like a station master, he liked it and what Gabriel liked, Gabriel got. Gabriel was a man with responsibilities. He had lost most of his free time, he no longer had the opportunity to practice the trumpet, but then he was the head of one of the largest organisation in the world. He wasn't the absolute head of course, they were still over seen by the Big Man, the creator of the organisation but Gabriel had to deal with most of the day to day hassles; the endless meetings. The lift doors slid open and he walked into the expectant hush of the board room. Senior managers muttered quietly between themselves as he progressed to the head of the table. The more ambitious greeted him and hoped he was well but today was not a good day to tempt fate for today was an emergency meeting. Something had gone wrong, very wrong indeed.

He lowered himself into his executive leather chair, reached for the water which was in a container that always reminded him of a specimen bottle, and waited for the silence. He gave a silent nod to Michael who was sitting to his right. They shared the responsibility of the organisation and yet Michael always seemed to look so relaxed. He sat there now, one foot resting on the other knee, flicking through messages on his phone. He was probably making arrangements for tonight. Gabriel vaguely remembered the times when he had had free evenings. He pulled his attention back to the now silent table. He steepled his fingers and sat back in his chair letting his gaze scan down the two columns of expectant faces until he located the man he was after.

"Jenkins." The head of monitoring snapped to attention. "I wonder if you would care to brief everybody on the matter that you brought to my attention this afternoon."

"Certainly Sir." He jumped from his seat and almost trotted to the front of the room and took up a position by the side of a large screen. Gabriel spun around to face him. He had heard it before obviously but it was probably best if the managers could not see his expression as he heard the news again.

"If the lights could be dimmed and I could have the first slide." The room was flooded with a pale orange glow from the screen. "This is the Dali Lama, the spiritual leader of Tibet." There was a general murmur around the table. "Every time his Earthly body dies his spirit is reincarnated to the village at the bottom of the mountain on which he has his residence. That is correct isn't it?" Jenkins searched the table for a colleague. A man in the dark recesses of the far end leant forward.

"That's a bit of an over simplification but essentially yes that is right, twenty four times so far." It was Henderson, head of reincarnation.

"This last happened eighteen years ago." Jenkins moved his slides on to a picture of a Tibetan funeral followed by a cartoon of a mountain and the village showing the spiritual flow. He waved again and a list of names appeared on the screen. "These are a small selection of the souls that we have to monitor, obviously starting with the big boys like the Anti-Christ and going right down to Kevin Gungy. We have an equal number of positive souls to keep an eye on too. Now..."

He waved again and a budget sheet kept up. Gabriel made a mental note that despite his express instruction to not link this too resource, Jenkins appeared to be about to do so. "As you will know, monitoring was amalgamated with intentions a few years ago in a hope to add a forecasting feature to the monitoring and this has eaten heavily into the budget." He pointed to the large section on the pie chart. "The result is that we have had to cut down on the number of occasions each soul is monitored. Jenkins put on a very grave face. "I feel this is what has led to the current situation."

"Which is?" Prompted Gabriel.

"We have lost the Dali Lama." There was a general snigger around the table and Gabriel was aware that Michael had muttered something under his breath. "We were monitoring at the point of reincarnation and he was defiantly in that village. Ten years later he was defiantly in Tibet and last week when he stopped off at Heathrow on his way to Washington, we got a positive reading in London. Jenkins quickly flicked through several screens that appeared to show a monitoring screen with dots on and dates in the top corner. "The problem is we still have a positive reading in London and the Dali Lama is in Washington."

Gabriel span his chair around to face the table again.

"The problem gentlemen is that we now have this." He flicked his fingers and the screen behind him changed to something that looked like a meteorological map of America. The east half was covered with a purple haze containing odd spots of pink. "Bad intentions gentlemen." He flicked his fingers and it zoomed in over Washington. "and it gets darker the further you zoom in." He paused and looked around the table. His eyes rested on Michael and they had a silent conversation as to the problems with staff. "Suggestions gentlemen?"

"Do we not have record facilities on the monitoring. Could we not find out what the Dali Lana's soul was doing whilst we weren't looking?" A bright spark at the far end thrust his hand up.

"They have only just been installed." Jenkins returned to his place at the table, adverting his gaze from his colleagues. Gabriel hadn't appeared angry when he had told him about the situation that afternoon, and he didn't appear too angry just now but in some ways this controlled flat emotion was ten times worse than shouting.

"Are we saying that the person in Washington that looks like the Dali Lama does not contain his soul?" Michael sought some verification.

"That is what we are saying." Gabriel sat back and looked at his partner. Although the room was full of senior managers they both knew any solution was probably going to come from them. ". The problem is that this so called Dali Lama has a private meeting with the President of the United States, and I," Gabriel raised himself from his seat and walked over to the screen, "do not like the look of this. We haven't seen anything this size since 2001."

"It seems clear to me." Michael sat back and lifted his feet up so that his crossed ankles rested lightly on the edge of the table. Here was a man who oozed confidence, ever since he had picked up his first flaming sword. "You're going to have to send in an Angel, someone who can actually get the job done."

"I think you might be right." Gabriel looked at the slide again, that darkness was worrying him.

"Oh, I am, and I have just the man."

6

"Jayne Pottage!" The curly haired woman shouted the name into the filled waiting room. "Jayne Pottage."

"Here." Jayne rushed across waving her form. She had been sitting on the hard plastic chair for what seemed like hours since the ambulance men had dropped her at the door of the sorting centre. She had double checked twice that she was meant to just wait. There was a general murmur over the whole room but there didn't seem to be any specific conversations. What would you say to someone? Sorry to hear about your loss? The vast room had an air of incredulity about it; no one really believed that they were there.

The woman beamed a smile and stood back to allow her through into what turned out to be a very small interview room.

"Take a seat, sorry about the delay but you'll not find too many people complaining. This isn't the sort of place where you want to start upsetting people." She stared into Jayne's blank face. "Well, could go either way." She made a little motion with her hand indicating a fine balance. "Now, I see you've got a form with you." She took it from Jayne's hand, "Always saves time." She scanned down the form. "Ah, it was Patrick." She indicated a chair to Jayne. "He's a dear. Now I'll just need to ask you a few more questions." She sat down opposite Jayne and smiled again.

"Religion?"

"Church of England." It was what she had been baptised into but Jayne couldn't actually remember the last time she had seen the inside of a church. The woman ticked a box on the sheet.

"Always good to have a religion, atheist's corner is beginning to fill up."

"Atheist's corner?" Jayne queried.

"Well, there is nothing we can do with them until they come to terms with the situation. Poor dears, some of them have been sitting there for an awfully long time. Now..." she looked back at the form, "Church of England you say. Is there anything you would like to confess? Only, we have to ask. We get regular up dates from the Catholics of course but nothing from the rest of you Christians." She smiled across at Jayne.

"I don't think so."

"Good, good." She balanced a set of glasses on the end of her nose. "Ever broken any of the Ten Commandments. They are displayed on a plaque on the wall if you are not sure of them." She indicated over her shoulder with the end of her pen. Jayne read down the list.

"I think I might have killed someone."

"And you didn't think that came under 'anything to confess'?" The woman momentarily stopped her box ticking and peered over her glasses.

"Well, I don't know. I got killed in a car crash which was my fault and I think other people were involved..."

"Hold on." The woman put her pen down and pulled out a little keyboard from under the desk. "No point getting hysterical about it. Let's check it out." She pulled the form over towards her and typed in a few details. "Alright, you were killed in a car accident in Aylesbury."

"No, on the North circular."

"Records, you can't trust them with anything." She handed the form back to Jayne. "If you want to just give me a moment I'll see if we can get this sorted." She pointed to a small door in the other wall of the office. "If you take a seat through there, we will give you a shout in a minute."

7

"Explain it to me again." Joshua was feeling harassed. He had a large section to run and he didn't need hassle like this especially today, his wedding anniversary - which he had forgotten about until about 30 minutes ago. "You see the problem I have." He continued without waiting for an explanation, "I can't quite grasp what the hell you were doing there armed with..." he lifted up the clipboard on which his notes were written, "two pence, a packet of gum and a ruler."

"Four pence."

"What?"

"It was four pence. You said two pence." Martin , a picture of calmness and serenity, sat in the chair opposite the fuming Joshua.

"Does it really matter." Joshua threw the clipboard onto the desk. "Do you know the size of our arms budget? We spend a bloody fortune on the latest hi tech stuff for you guys. We don't expect you to go out armed with just a trumpet these days so why do you continue to do it?"

"I hadn't been planning to do it."

"Oh well, thank the Lord for that." Joshua stalked to his drinks cabinet and poured himself a large drink. "We would be in real trouble if you had planned to do it." He took a swig and let the liquor trickle down his throat. He really must get in touch with Doug and see how he was feeling. He needed to persuade him to take back the responsibility for these angel teams.

"Did the deal come off?" The question came from behind him.

"You know darn well it didn't. There was no drugs deal. The whole lot got lost at sea so, you did it again. You screwed up completely and still managed to succeed." He downed the rest of the drink. "Why can't you just stick to the plan Martin, it would be so much easier." He returned to his seat behind his desk and sat down.

"It wouldn't be so much fun though." Martin tried a weak grin. You couldn't really help but smile back. He had a friendly face, a youthful appearance and just a faint devil may care attitude. He sat opposite the smartly dressed Joshua in jeans and a lumber jack shirt and he didn't feel in the least bit intimidated. There was a knock on the door and Simon walked in.

"Sorry I'm late Sir." He pulled a chair over.

"That's alright Simon." Joshua produced a beige folder from the lower drawer of his desk. He laid it on his desk and placed his hands on top of it. "I was kind of hoping that you might have been transferred back to your original line management by now."

"I'm sure it won't be long." Simon looked at Martin and gave a subtle nod that implied he was waiting for a similar comment from him.

"We should get the old team back together." Joshua looked at him from underneath his eyebrows. It was the first comment he remembered Martin making about Doug. He let a faint glimmer of hope ignite. Might he soon hand back the responsibility for this pair?

"Well we can work on that but for now I have one simple little job that I need you to do. It's nice and straight forward, no breaking into cars, nothing like that. I just want you to take a trip to Washington and find this man." He took a photo out of the file, turned it around and laid it on the desk in front of Martin and Simon. They lent in to look at it.

"The Dali lama?"

"Well spotted Martin."

"I thought he lived in Tibet."

"He's over in the US for a Presidential meeting. All the leaders of the major religions were invited." Simon lifted up the photo and squinted at it. "Besides, he's been in exile from Tibet for years."

"Well, at least one of you keeps up to date." Joshua took the photo back and placed it in the folder.

"You want us to just go and find him?"

"Well yes. It shouldn't be too difficult because this is the address he is staying at." Joshua clipped the paper note to the photo. "I just want you to go there, get a positive ID and report back."

"Why?" Martin relaxed back into his chair.

"You are a field operative Martin. I am one of the senior managers of external activity who, because of the current indisposition of your boss, has the pleasure of looking after you two. You are going to do it because I told you to." Joshua wondered about going for a second drink.

"Something is up, isn't it." Martin slowly smirked.

"Something is up." Joshua shut the folder and handed it across to Simon with a small smile. "And I want you to go down and do this for me. I want a positive ID before the full briefing. The complete details are in the folder. I don't know how you are going to do it because security is as tight as a drum and, to be honest, I don't really care how you do it but talk to Hans because we have problems with teleport and projection at the moment - too many deities in one place." Joshua pushed his chair a little way back from the desk.

"I'll give you three days. I'll arrange a briefing for three o'clock on the fourth day, just to give you a little leeway." He tapped both his hands on the desktop and smiled. "You're wasting time gentlemen."

8

"Hello. Are you OK?" It took a while for Jayne to realize that this question was addressed to her. "It's just you look a little...dishevelled." She let the comment wash over her before replying. Considering what she had been through today dishevelled was probably quite good. She lifted her head from her hands and looked at the shoes of her inquisitor.

They were black smart shoes. Oxfords, if her memory served her right, although it looked like they hadn't seen polish in the last few days, possibly weeks. The trousers were just a bit too long, sitting on top of the shoes. They were smart trousers. The kind, that according to Jayne's Mum, should have a crease up the front of them although whenever her mother tried it she always ended up with two parallel creases within a few washes due to the incompetence of the ironer. The trousers sat just a bit too low on the hips, almost like the occupant had lost weight since he had last worn them, which might have accounted for them being a bit too long. The shirt was barely tucked in on one side and the other side had clearly just been pushed back in to place. The tie was slid a few inches down the shirt front and was that aubergine? A funny colour for a tie. Jayne couldn't remember ever seeing anything like it before. The top two shirt buttons were undone. There was a jacket, pushed back behind the hands that were stuck into the trouser pockets. There was something about the whole ensemble that said European rather than British. By the time she got to the face she clearly had an expression that was similar to 'pot calling the kettle black'. With a wave of one hand he captured his entire costume.

"I know, that's how I recognize it in others." The face broke in to a grin that it was impossible to ignore. There was a faint accent but she couldn't place it.

"There is some problem with my paperwork." Jayne pointed over towards the officials who had just directed her to this waiting area.

"Can I get you a coffee whilst you wait?"

"I was told to wait here." She smiled up at him. A coffee would be great but she didn't want to jeopardize the process. It seemed to consist of a lot of brief questions and a lot of sitting and waiting. If she missed her name being called she had a feeling it might add hours onto the process. He pulled his tie up, doing up one of the buttons on the way, turned and waved at the man who had just spoken to Jayne. He came trotting over.

"Hi, I'm going to take...this lady."

"Jayne." Jayne prompted. He started again

"I'm going to take Jayne over to the cafe for a coffee. We are going to be twenty to thirty minutes. Could you bring her completed paperwork over to us before we finish."

"I can try but," Jayne couldn't see the exchange of facial expressions that clearly took place. "I'll bring it over." The man rearranged a few things on his clip board and returned to his desk.

"Coffee?" The stranger indicated the cafe with his hand and raised a questioning eyebrow.

"I'd be delighted." Jayne got to her feet and led the way to the cafe. Maybe the day wasn't quite as bad as she thought

Jayne shifted the chair out of the way and eased herself into the alcove at the front of the coffee shop, slightly regretting that she had asked the stranger to surprise her with a drink. She could do with something familiar on such a strange day, even if it was only her favourite coffee. Although, given their current tax arrangements, Jayne very much doubted that her favourite coffee franchise had made it to heaven. She lowered her head to run her hands through her hair. When she opened her eyes she was faced with the frothy milk top and familiar caramel drizzle lines.

She flinched a little.

"I'm sorry, was that not the sort of surprise you were expecting?" He lowered himself into the chair opposite with a very small espresso and a glass of water in front of him.

"No, no, it's fantastic. Thank you." She picked up the cup and took a sip of the froth and drizzle.

"So, do you usually hang around here offering people coffee?

"No," he grinned again. The complete disarming welcoming expression that she sought. "You caught me on an off day. I work just around the corner and I'm meant to be meeting someone here in an hour. I thought I would make an exception for you because you looked so..."

"Dishevelled?" Jayne prompted.

"Dishevelled." He took a mouthful of coffee. " I didn't mean to be rude, you just looked like you could do with a coffee."

"It's been a strange sort of day." Jayne took a mouthful of froth and looked out at the busy arrivals hall. "I never thought it would be like this."

"You weren't expecting to end up here then?"

"No!" What sort of question was that. She looked at him as if he had gone mad.

"Well, it could have been a long illness or something." He sat back and relaxed, took a mouthful of coffee and looked out across the arrival hall. He never tired of sitting here watching people arrive. The whole range of emotions from relief to denial. You saw them all in the arrival hall.

"No, car accident." She raised a questioning eyebrow which she thought could be read as asking him how he came to be here. She wasn't used to asking people how they had died.

"Oh, sorry." He caught her expression as his gaze came back to the table. "Erm... stabbed."

"Oh, nasty."

"Yes, it smarted a bit at the time." Without thinking he rubbed his hand across his chest and Jayne wondered if that was the site of the wound.

"Have you been here long?" Jayne didn't need the derisive snort of laughter from the stranger to know that that was a strange question. Maybe slightly better than the archetypal 'Do you come here often' but not a lot.

"I'm sorry. I didn't mean to be rude. I know it's hard to adjust when you first arrive here." He tried a smile but Jayne was too busy staring at her coffee cup to notice.

"I have no idea what to do." A slight wail entered her voice. "What am I meant to do, ask you what you do for a living? You're dead! I'm dead! I wasn't expecting this." She took in the whole waiting area with a wave of her hand.

"I know. It's hard." He held his hands out in the classic calm down pose. "My advice, for what it's worth, try to carry on as normally as you can whilst you come to terms with it. You'll get asked what you want to do. Opt to work, keep yourself busy whilst you sort your head out. Oh, here he comes." The stranger got to his feet as the official trotted over with a pile of papers.

"Here we are Miss Pottage." He handed them over. "If you want to follow me we have found a space with an advisor who can see you right away." He took a step back and indicated the way with a big flourish. Jayne got up and grabbed her jacket.

"Well, thanks for the coffee. It was nice to meet you."

"The pleasure was all mine." They shook hands and she stepped forward with the official, only realizing she hadn't asked the stranger's name as she entered the advisor's office.

9

"You're late." Simon looked up from his lap top as Doug entered the coffee shop.

"Yeah, I'm sorry. I had to duck into arrivals." Doug slid into the chair opposite Simon and waved across at one of the waiters.

"Were you followed again?" Simon glanced back down at the document and then peered over the screen at Doug. "This has got to stop. It's getting ridiculous. What is that now, two months?"

"It's probably nearer three. It would be annoying if it weren't so laughable. It's easy to give them the slip. I popped into Arrivals and even had time for a coffee with some random auburn haired girl."

Simon slowly shut the lap top.

"Random girls are either dark or blonde. No random girl is auburn." Doug grinned.

"Ok, maybe she wasn't that random, and maybe it was nearer brown."

Simon mirrored his grin.

"Good to see you are starting to think about getting back to normal." He sat back as the waiter laid down another two coffees in front of them, taking Simon's earlier empty cup away with him.

"Yeah well, small steps. I didn't even get her details." Doug pulled a pad out of his jacket pocket. "Anyway, can you get me up to speed?"

"Are you coming back?" Simon took a mouthful out of his coffee.

"I need to get back to work Si. This sitting behind a desk is not for me. I miss meeting up in random places, watching the goings on down below. I miss the people." Doug took a drink of his coffee and noted the amount of espresso he was drinking. He would have trouble sleeping tonight. "I was screwed over by some people I thought could be trusted and now I'm being followed. I want to get some normality back in my life."

"I think that might be the first time we have been described as normal. Joshua was giving Martin a bit of a dressing down today for the last screw up." Simon pulled the beige folder out of his lap top case. "I waited outside his office to let him finish before I went in to get this." He slid the folder across the table. "Our latest mission." Doug opened the folder and flicked through the pages. He looked at Simon, raising a quizzical eyebrow.

"Go and photograph the Dali Lama?"

"Yep."

"Something is up."

"Yep."

10

"Jayne Pottage, Muriel Clegg and Peter Cranworth." The bus stopped again at the side of another street. The brightly dressed young man holding the microphone handed them each a large cardboard folder. "If you go into reception here, they will show you to your apartments." He waited whilst they stepped off of the bus and then waved as the doors closed and the bus moved off.

"Wow - this is great." Muriel, a large coloured woman looked around them. The sun was shining, the pavement was clean and the birds were singing. "Anyone would think we were in heaven." With a hearty laugh at her own joke she waddled inside followed by her two speechless companions.

Jayne had taken the strangers advise when she had been called back into the room at the sorting centre. She had opted to be town based and to get a job as soon as possible. The computer had identified a number of openings. She had said she would be happy to do anything for now and they had said they would be in touch. Quite how they would be in touch she didn't know.

The apartment was fantastic, the sort of thing she would never have been able to afford on Earth. The full height windows flooded the space with light and it appeared to have all the mod cons including several gadgets that Jayne had no idea what they were. Lying on the coffee table was another folder entitled 'city guide'. Inside that Jayne found a restaurant guide, cinema listings, entertainment section, it seemed endless. She wondered if there was anything in the kitchen, maybe the stuff to make a cup of tea. The guide hadn't mentioned anything about shopping. On opening the first cupboard in the kitchen, Jayne discovered it was fully stocked with all of her favourite foods. The fridge was bursting at the seams with all the food she used to think about buying but could never afford and on the door were two little fridge magnets just like the ones in her own kitchen. There was a particularly cute one of a clown juggling and underneath that was a little note. 'Training starts tomorrow at 9am, Angel HQ.' Jayne thought it was ironic that it had taken her dying for her life to start coming together.

11

"Hans my little buddy." Martin sat down on top of a pile of paperwork on the edge of the semi circular desk. The blond cropped young man peered over the top of his glasses as though he actually had to check who was referring to him in such a manner.

"I've told Joshua it can't be done." He returned to staring intently at the screen in front of him.

"Well, what can you do?" We've got to get to Washington." Hans spun around in his swivel chair and looked from Martin to Simon and back to Martin.

"I can get you down to the city limits." He pointed at Martin. "You will have to make your own way in, but you." He turned to Simon, "I can't project you any further in."

"City limits? You're joking!" Simon gave him an exasperated look.

"Hold on Hans, what if he was inside me."

"No, no. I'm not doing that again." Simon still had flashbacks of the last time they had tried that. It hadn't gone well.

"It wouldn't help you. You could maybe go in a few extra miles but we could risk losing you both." Hans pushed his glasses further up his little button nose.

"What about voice? Can you give me voice contact all the way in?" Simon was reluctant to release Martin on the mission with no guiding influences. He didn't think that would be a wise move and he was fairly sure Joshua would never forgive him.

"Voice is no problem." Hans sat back with a smug little grin.

"You can't get me into our base in Washington?" Martin had assumed that he would be able to get in to the centre of the town. Having to travel in from the city limits would certainly add to the challenges.

"No, city limits is the best I can offer." Hans folded his arms across his chest.

"You'll have to go to the limits and work your way in." Simon looked across at Martin.

"Do we have time?" Martin turned back to Hans. "Am I right in thinking I would have to get back to the city limits to get out?"

"It would be a risk not to, it all depends on where you are going to be in relation to the deities."

"I'm going to be standing next to the Dali Lama."

"City limits." Hans twiddled a few knobs in front of his array of screens. Simon pulled Martin a few feet back from the screens and dropped his voice to a whisper.

"What are we going to do? You are going to have to get in to town, identify the Dali Lama and get out in three days. There has got to be a way around this." Simon walked back to Hans and his impressive array of screens. "There isn't any area of Washington that these deities aren't affecting?"

"There are two weak patches. One to the north over an active coven and one to the east over a devil worshipping sect but I would advise against it." Hans quickly zoomed in and out of the screen areas showing Simon the various locations. "They are not that weak and we could lose your signal at any time. On top of that the place is crawling with FBI men, if anything out of the ordinary happens anywhere these boys are going to spot it."

"An active coven and devil worship count as ordinary these days do they?"

"It is Washington." Hans retorted.

"What do you reckon Martin?" They both looked across to their silent partner.

"Can you trace someone on this stuff?" Martin waved towards the screens and computers.

"Of course." Hans seemed a little affronted by the question.

"Alright, can you find Charlie Chatney, number..." Martin paused, "I can't remember, but it ends 793N."

"That's it?" Hans typed away. "That's all of the number you have got?"

"'Fraid so."

"Give me a clue." Hans stared into a screen full of data that was scrolling past his eyes. "Where are you expecting him to be?"

"America, hopefully heading towards Washington." There was a few minutes of silence as data rolled up the screen so fast that Simona and Martin were not sure how Hans was even checking it.

"Got him." Hans flicked to the maps and zoomed in and in. "You lucky bastard. He is about fifty miles outside the city limits and closing."

"Is he alone?" Hans pushed himself to another screen to answer Martin's question.

"There is another life form, but I wouldn't say it was human."

"You've met his wife then." There was a quiet murmur of a suppressed laugh even though they knew they shouldn't be laughing at Martin's joke.

"It's probably a dog." Hans concluded.

"That's what I thought the first time but no, it's defiantly his wife." Martin jumped down from his perch on Hans' desk. "Ok Hans, send me down. I want voice from Simon, and Simon." He turned to his friend "anything I say, try and arrange the back up."

"Ok." Simon nodded, "but try and be reasonable this time."

"Ok Hans, can you put me down at the next diner along that road and make sure he stops at it."

"No problem." Hans, now in his element, flicked switched, twiddled knobs and entered coordinates. "Alright." He looked across to Martin for some signal. He got a thumbs up. "Going now." Martin vanished. Hans turned around to Simon. "Now, let's get you a mike."

12

The foyer area of Angels HQ was exactly what you would expect if you had thought about it for a while. It always caught people unawares to start with but then most of them had just suffered a death in the family, namely their own, and they were just getting used to the idea that there was something afterwards. They were not, generally speaking, in the mood for analysing what they would, or would not, expect in the foyer of a large organisation. If you walked into any large bank head office in any major town you would expect to see an impressive sight. Maybe a little impersonal with lots of efficient looking people and daunting decor, imagine how many people that bank would employ. In fact, why not imagine how many people there are on Earth. Now imagine how many people have ever died. Even if you divide that number by two to account for the people who have gone 'the other way' and aren't in the vicinity of Angels HQ, there are still a lot more dead people than there are alive. Alright, they are not all angels but there was no getting around the fact that Angels HQ must employ a lot of people.

Jayne was suitable impressed as she sat in the deep leather seats of the entrance hall. She had found a suit in the wardrobe of her new apartment which had fitted her perfectly. The kitchen cupboards had contained all her favourite foods, the TV programmes had been her favourites and it was slowly dawning on her that maybe it was going to be like this for ever. Was she always going to have exactly what she wanted? And if so, where was the man of her dreams that she had never found on Earth? She hadn't really been prepared for death, not in this sense anyway. The religious classes at school had always been some long winded meta physical discussion as to whether God existed or not. They didn't cover the things you needed to know; can you eat cream cakes once you are dead without putting on weight? Can you kill yourself once you are already dead? She had found a book last night that dealt with some of the technicalities; how to appeal if you thought you were unjustly killed, applications for visitation rights, requests for haunting - that sort of thing but no actual explanations of what being dead entails. Not that it really mattered as Jayne had decided, after much thought last night, that she must be in a coma in a hospital somewhere and this was all some mad dream that she was going to wake up from at some point.

"Jayne Pottage?"

"Yes." She tried to wriggle to the front of the seat but, as always with leather furniture, it was designed for maximum embarrassment.

"If you would care to take the lift up to the second floor. The rest of the group have already gone up. Your name wasn't on the list for some reason." The bespectacled receptionist took a step back and indicated the lifts at the end of the hall. She stood there politely as Jayne struggled to her feet and then patted the chair back into shape as Jayne walked towards the lifts.

Lecture hall two was already in darkness when Jayne found her way there. No one was talking so she slipped in through the back door and took a seat at the end of the last row. The man at the front of the room peered up at her over the top of his glasses.

"Jayne Pottage?" He waited for her to reply. "Do come down here girl. Entirely my fault I'm afraid. You weren't on the list, but no need to hide at the back, come down and join us." He waved her down to the front where four other people were sitting. It looked like the class from Hell. If you could imagine four very swotty looking people and a very patronising teacher then you would have the scene. Add to this two suited men sitting in the gloom behind the spot lighted teacher and another perched on the front row of the desks not paying any attention to proceedings.

"I take it you won't have received a set of notes either." He handed her a thick folder "I'm Dickson, Head of Training." He pushed his glasses further up his nose, and indicated for Jayne to sit down. "Now everybody." He addressed the whole room even though it was only the first row that was occupied. "You are about to begin a training course that will bring you to the point of junior management. In time you will each be in charge of a field operative, or angel as they used to be called, maybe even a team of them." Smug grin. "The training is split into several sections." He flicked up a slide. "Basic ethical training; what you are allowed to do, how far you can go. Projection training; getting used to the transportation system and understanding the physics behind it. Reporting; the correct way to go about filing reports..." his voice droned on. Jayne lifted the cover off of the notes and flicked through the first few pages.

"Miss Pottage. I'm not talking for my own health. You have a question I'm not addressing?" Jayne looked up to find the hook nose and hawk eyes in front of her.

"I was just wondering what form do these angels take on Earth." Jayne quickly made up a question rather than be brow beaten by this intimidating teacher. She hadn't quite recovered from being referred to as 'girl'.

"Exactly the same form as everybody else. It wouldn't be much use if they stood out from the crowd would it." He pulled himself erect and strutted back to his podium, casting his eye over the other students to make sure they had noted his put down.

"So how can you tell them apart?" Jayne called after him.

"Well, they're dead. That's always a bit of a giveaway." He waited for the expected sniggers from the two men in the gloom behind him. The man perched at the end looked over his shoulder towards her. Jayne sat back in the hard wooden seat. Maybe heaven wasn't such a good place after all. Dickson droned on for just over the hour before announcing it was time for coffee and disappearing.

The staff room, as it was labelled, didn't take much finding, you could just follow the aroma of freshly ground coffee all the way to the counter. Jayne's swotty classmates were ensconced around a table with their notes open and bottles of mineral water. She took her coffee and wandered over to the window. Just then Dickson blustered into the room followed by the two men from the gloom. Sauntering behind was the man who had been perched on the desk at the front of the room. Now, out in the daylight, Jayne was sure that this was the person from the coffee shop yesterday. He raised a hand casually acknowledging her and broke into a grin. Having got his coffee, he negotiated a path through the chairs towards her window.

"We meet again."

"I took your advice, got a job."

"It's a bit unusual to come straight here. We usually have people who have been around for a few years." He nodded over towards the table where her classmates sat.

"Do you hand pick them so you just get people who think physics and form filling are fun?" The was no outward sign but Jayne could tell from the way his shoulders moved up and down that he was trying to suppress a laugh. He rubbed his fingers down his cheeks to the point of his chin, almost deliberately trying to wipe the smile off his face.

"That was a good question, to make up on the spot." A compliment but also a warning that he was on to her lack of attention.

"He didn't seem to think so." They both looked across the room towards Dickson for a second and then returned to gazing out of the window.

"That's because he is an arse." Jayne was not as successful at suppressing her laugh and a small noise escaped. Everybody in the room turned to look. "Shall we take a seat?" He walked over towards a sofa and waited for Jayne to sit down before sitting opposite. "Hi." He extended his hand, "I'm Doug."

13

The interstate to Washington is one of those boring American roads that you see in the movies; completely straight in both directions with the odd building placed alongside. Charlie had been travelling down it all day. He was meant to be on holiday, fishing up at the lake, but he had been called in as back up for this Presidential meeting. He needlessly glanced in the mirror. He was getting near enough to Washington now that he would expect a little more traffic. He passed through a small settlement that seemed to sprawl more than the others.

"Must be getting close boy." He addressed the animal curled up on the passenger seat. It raised one eyebrow and returned to its snooze. Benji - that was the dog's name, went everywhere with Charlie. He had been the only non contested item in a rather sordid custody battle with his ex-wife, but that was all water under the bridge now. Street lights stated to appear. "What do you say to a snack stop Benji?" Charlie paused as though actually expecting a reply. "We will pull in at the next place." No sooner had he said those words than a diner appeared - his prayers had been answered.

The diner looked pretty full, which was a bit of a surprise considering the car park was half empty. Charlie looked around the tables. There was a spare chair but it was sharing with a very large bespectacled woman with a small dog that looked more like a rat on a piece of string. He glanced down the counter and spied a free chair at the end.

"Coffee please Miss." He caught the waitress' eye as she passed for the fourth time and she smiled sweetly in acceptance of the order. After wiping the stains off of the menu card, he gave it a glance. He didn't want fish, that would remind him too much of the holiday he was missing and he wasn't really hungry enough for a whole steak. He would just have a burger. The waitress was involved with another customer a few chairs down, she seemed to be having a hard time.

"That is not an option Sir; it's sunny side up or not."

"What do you mean it's not an option. All I'm asking is for a little fat to be flicked on top of the egg rather than turning the whole thing upside down."

"I'll see what I can do." She promised in a way that assured you she would do nothing. Charlie leant back on his stool. He had heard an order like that before. If his suspicions were right he should now hear 'Coke with no ice.'"

"And a coke please, with no ice."

"Martin?" Charlie peered down the counter. A head appeared, looking the other way, it slowly turned around.

"Charlie! What a surprise." After a short negotiation, Martin swapped chairs with the man between them and they resumed their greetings.

"What are you doing here? I haven't heard from you since that deal down in Denver." Charlie passed his order over to the waitress.

"Yeah, I had to fly after that. You been keeping busy? How is Janice?"

"We split up last year."

"Oh." Martin's sails collapsed temporarily. "Still, more time for the fishing." He reached over and grabbed his plate as it was placed at his original seat. Charlie tried a small smile.

"I would have if it wasn't for this Presidential meeting."

"You haven't been called in as well have you?" It wasn't often that Martin counted his blessings but seeing the change in Charlie that a few years could make, he was counting them now. The man had been so full of life, a young thirty five. Now he seemed an ancient thirty seven, very cynical and depressed.

"Yes, called in as back up. How much back up do you need for heaven's sake? It's a bunch of religious leaders not terrorists or politicians." Charlie's burger arrived. "What is vice's interest?"

Ah yes, vice. Martin couldn't quite remember what he had told Charlie last time and that had been long before he was convinced of the value of notes. Vice was a pretty safe bet; you could get into most places with that. Nowhere was immune from vice and claiming to be under cover obtained you access to some pretty far out places too. Added to that, Martin quite liked it because it wasn't too far away from the truth. It had been handy in the early years but by now he was such an accomplished liar he rarely fell back on the truth.

"We've heard that some of the extreme groups are arranging some sort of scaremongering tactic." Did that make sense? Charlie seemed to think so as he nodded knowingly.

"So you're going all the way to HQ?"

"Yep, got to meet up with..." Martin looked blankly into space.

"Morgan?" Charlie prompted.

"Of course, Morgan. He should be expecting me." Oh thanks, said a little voice in Martin's head, call that reasonable? "Only the stupid car has broken down."

"I could give you a lift in if you want. I've got to report to Morgan myself." Charlie downed his coffee.

"Have you? That would be great. The car people are coming out tomorrow to tow it in."

"No problem."

"Great. I'll just go to the loo." Martin hopped down off of his stool and darted across to the toilet. He got in and leant back against the door and grinned. "Did you hear that Si? We're in."

14

There is a big difference between arriving in Washington and actually seeing the Dali Lama, a fact that Martin had been reminding himself of all the way into town. He wasn't helped by Simon's voice in his head asking him exactly what he planned to do. He didn't plan to do anything. Generally, he never planned to do anything, it all just seemed to happen around him. The last time he went in with a plan it hadn't really worked. He tried not to brood over that one.

Martin wasn't familiar with Washington so he didn't even bother to try and keep track of where he was. Charlie had taken so many wrong terms they could have been anywhere.

"I think it should be on the next block." Charlie peered down at the photocopied map he had been sent. Benji had had a go at one corner and a couple of coffee rings had obscured part of it but he was fairly sure that they were close.

He turned the corner to come face to face with a barrier across the road.

"Chatney, FBI." He flicked open his wallet as the guard looked into the car. Martin did likewise and prayed it was no longer an ID card for London transport. Prayer is a powerful thing if you are an angel, especially if you have got support like Simon, who had foreseen the problem a couple of hours ago.

"It's upside down Sir." Martin flicked it over without even looking; studying your own ID card was always a give away. If Simon can produce ID cards, Martin thought, why couldn't he produce car keys? Then maybe they would be on a decent assignment not looking for the Dali Lama.

'Oh no you don't.' Came a voice in his head. 'Don't try and blame that one on me.' There were times when thought communication had its bad points.

The barrier swung up and they drove through into the car park of the police academy at which the FBI operation was based. The place was alive with uniformly dressed men. They were jogging around in packs chanting, banging riot shields, letting off water canon and lots of other things that Martin didn't want to study too closely. They parked their car and made their way inside.

"Help Hans." The shout went up in the darkened control room and Hans, complete with swivel chair, wheeled into view. Simon had always wondered why the lights were so dim in the control room. Hans said it was so that you could see red warning lights more easily but that seemed a thin excuse. Simon had his suspicions that it was just an exaggerated sense of the dramatic.

"What's up?" Hans arrived at the consul beside him. They were in a little alcove off of the main room. Usually operatives clocked in and out at set times so the counsels were only in use for short bursts of time. This alcove was set up for continuous monitoring missions like this. Hans clipped an ear piece onto his head set.

"He is about to walk into a room of FBI agents who are meant to be expecting him." Simon twiddled a few knobs. "I'm not sure I've got his believability strong enough."

"How close are we to the deities?" Hans flicked the adjacent screen into life.

"Not close. He's at the police HQ."

"Does he have good ID?" Hans twiddled a few knobs at the side of the screen.

"No, it's holographic."

"Have you thrown a net?"

"Thrown a net?" Simon turned to look at Hans, Hans just rolled his eyes up to the ceiling.

"We will have to work fast." He began punching in coordinates, dialing up numbers and flicking through screens. "Bring it up on the big screen." Simon could cope with that command. He flicked a switch and the transparent screen behind them came to life. It showed green lines for solid objects, green blobs for life forms and two red blobs just entering the building. They were Martin and Charlie, red because they were tagged.

"Well at least we can see them all. We've been having some issues recently." Hans shook his head. "Have you identified the room?"

"Not verbally, but I think it is top right." Simon pointed up to the small room full of green blobs.

"Slow him down." Simon lowered his mike and, back on Earth, Martin remembered he had left his ID in the car.

"I don't know if this is going to work." Hans sped backwards to the counsels on the other side of Simon. "It's not a great area with all those deities, and things have been playing up. Can you lock a transporter onto Martins signal, just in case?"

"I thought you said the transporters wouldn't work." Simon pulled out a drawer and pressed in the coordinates. Transporter controls were kept out of view so that they couldn't be pressed accidentally.

"It won't, not 100%, but we can always get him back out of the atmosphere if we have to. If the net doesn't hold he will be in a room full of hostile FBI agents. They could take him to places we would never recover him from." Hans frantically pressed a few more controls. The two red blobs were once more proceeding up the corridor. "Ok, I'm keeping the net small. It should just cover that room, but I'm not sure how long I'll be able to hold it. How long do you think he will be in there?"

"It could be minutes, it could be hours."

"If it's hours, he is on his own. I'm just casting a thin believable net. Everyone in the room should have some faint belief that they are expecting him." The two red blobs stopped momentarily by a green line, behind which were a dozen green blobs. The green line began to move.

"Ok, casting now." Hans pressed the large red button in the centre of the panel and a faint blue circle appeared over the map of the room.

The man in the centre of the room looked up. He was hunched over a map of Washington, two colleagues on either side. He stared at the newcomers.

"Chatney, fish weren't biting then?" He tapped at a corner of the map and his four colleagues scribbled in the notebooks.

"No, sir." Charlie grudgingly added the second word.

"And you are?" Morgan redirected his stare to Martin.

"Martin Sir, Vice."

"Vice?" Morgan questioned it and then smirked. "You boys don't think one of our visitors is up to something surely?"

"Just here to check on a few extreme groups." There was silence, "Mr Morgan, Sir." Martin added.

"I don't recall being informed of vice's role in this." He turned to a man in the corner who was studying a clipboard full of papers.

"I can't seem to find a note of it Sir." Everyone in the room stiffened as he continued to flip through pages. "Ah yes, here it is Sir." The room relaxed. "Martin, vice. It's in your own handwriting Sir."

Nice touch, thought Martin.

"Well, what do you want?"

"Is it possible to get a list of all the visiting group and get clearance to join all of them?" Morgan stared at him for a few seconds.

"Are you vice too Chatney?" Morgan's eyes didn't leave Martin as he addressed the other man.

"Hell no Sir, just regular FBI." Charlie took a small step away from Martin. He didn't want to get caught in the cross fire.

"Fine, give him a list and a pass." Morgan returned to his maps as one of his underlings completed the relevant forms.

"Well thank you Sir." Martin took the offered papers and smiled. "I'll be on my way." As he left the room Morgan looked up from the map. He stared at the closed door for a few seconds.

"Willis."

"Sir." A muscular man who was needlessly wearing sunglasses stepped forwards. You could tell from the cut of his suit that he was armed. That or he had a very bad tailor.

"Follow him Willis. I don't trust him at all."

15

Jayne fiddled with the earring as she stared at herself in the mirror. She had always wanted a little black dress but she has never quite summoned by enough courage to wear one whilst she had been alive. She hadn't noticed it in the wardrobe that morning but when she started looking for something to wear to dinner she had found it hanging in with the shirts. She had her hair tied loosely back at the nape of her neck and even she had to admit she looked a million dollars. She was beginning to get the hang of this heaven thing how, or at least she thought she was. She finished with the earring, smoothed down the dress and picked up her jacket from the bed. She was ready at last, and it had only taken four hours.

When she finally arrived at the restaurant, it was only around the corner but she was new in town, Doug was waiting at the bar slowly sipping a drink that looked distinctly like whisky. He was probably trying to make it last.

"Sorry I'm late." She crept up behind him, suddenly doubting the decision over the dress.

"What's half an hour between friends." He looked stern to start with but seconds later his face split into a grin. "It's OK, they are holding our table." He guided her through the crowded restaurant to a small booth in the corner.

"Hey Dougie, nice to see you back." A velvet jacketed man approached the table with an extended hand. Doug jumped up to greet him.

"Hey Gino, nothing would keep me away from your restaurant. Let me introduce Jayne, she's a trainee over at HQ."

Gino bent down and lightly kissed her hand.

"Poaching the students now hey Dougie, a sure sign of being middle aged." He winked at Jayne and then sprung up as though a thought had struck him. "Hey kids, let me give you a night to remember. My chef has been working on some specials, very flashy. I'll give you a five course meal and you give me your opinions. What do you say?"

Doug offered the question across to Jayne.

"Sounds great." She beamed. Gino disappeared in a flurry of Italian commands.

"That is a very distinctive dress." Doug slid back into the seat.

"Don't you like it?"

"Oh, I love it. It's just not quite what I imagined you would wear." Jayne wasn't sure how to take that. A chat over coffee and he had already pigeon holed her as regards to clothes. Still, at least she had the ability to surprise.

"Well I thought, what the hell, it's not like anything bad is going to happen is it." The wine waiter showed them a bottle that meant nothing to Jayne. Doug waved him on to just pour the glasses.

"Bad things don't happen because of what your wear, but I'd be interested to hear your reasoning on this one." He slipped off his jacket and loosened his tie. He obviously wasn't that bothered about appearances. It had taken Jayne four hours to get ready and he had come straight from the office.

"You obviously don't walk down the same streets of London as I do." Jayne replied.

"Well, not in a little black dress." Doug smirked and then indicated that he still wanted to hear her reasoning.

"Well, this is heaven isn't it. Since I have arrived everything has gone just as I would have wanted it." Jayne blushed slightly as Doug raised a querying eyebrow to the word everything.

"You often find this." Doug twiddled the stem of his wine glass. "In the first few weeks even seemingly, intelligent people miss one of the basic concepts."

"Such as?" First the comment about the dress and now being described as 'seemingly intelligent'. Jayne was beginning to wonder whether she had missed his turn of phrase at the coffee break and whether she had just been bowled over by his smile and attention.

"Alright, let's suppose your idea of heaven is dinner with me." He rushed on because he was a genuinely modest man. "Suppose, purely hypothetically, especially in light of your last comment, but suppose dinner with you is my idea of hell. Now we are both in the same place but you are in heaven, and I am in hell." He looked across to make sure she had grasped the concept.

"You mean there are some nasty people out there."

"Not really nasty." He leant forward on to the edge of the table. "It's a lot harder to get into hell than you would think. If you were really evil then evil things happening to you might be your idea of heaven." Silence fell on the table.

"You mean." Jayne leant back as a selection of starters arrived. "That waiter over there could have been a waiter when he was alive and his idea of hell is to spend eternity in a busy restaurant whilst that waiter over there could have been a businessman whose idea of heaven is to wait on tables."

"Basically." Doug finished off his glass of wine as the wine waiter approached.

"So, Hell is not like Hell at all then." Jayne studied the dish in front of her. It looked beautiful, it smelt terrific and she couldn't wait to taste it.

"That depends on what your idea of Hell is."

"Screaming bodies, torture, boiling cauldrons, pitchforks, that sort of thing."

"No." Doug tucked into his food. Gino's restaurant was always busy. It was by far the best in town. Tables had to reserved weeks in advance, unless you knew the owner of course. "Don't get bogged down in the physics and geography of it." Doug punctuated the air with his fork. "All I'm saying is that it doesn't always go your way. They may be a time when you are geographically with someone but you don't perceive heaven as the same thing as them." He looked across the table at her. "How did we get into this from a comment about your dress?"

"I think you were trying to warn me about something." Jayne smirked back at him. He held the gaze for a minute, mumbled in agreement and then ate on.

"So when did you die Doug?"

"1565."

"Holy shit! Did you die young or don't you age here?" Doug stared at her, fork in mid air. He slowly chewed his mouthful, took a sip of wine and then replied.

"Both." He held the serious face for a few moments. "How young would I have had to have died to look like this nearly 500 years later? You don't age. You're dead, how can you age?"

"You keep saying that but we aren't acting like we're dead. Why are we eating if we're dead?" Just as Jayne thought she had understood it, something troubled her.

"Force of habit; you don't have to." Doug wiped his mouth and sat back in the seat. "That was great. I wonder what else

Gino has in store for us." He looked around the restaurant, it was another busy night.

"So Jayne, I take it from the accent that you are English."

"Yes, and you are..?"

"French originally but the accent was going before I died." A second course appeared in front of them. "This looks delicious." They both tucked in to the next course.

16

"Buddhists trip to see the Dali Lama?" Martin flipped open his ID as he approached the police guard.

"Over in the far corner Sir, just going through." The guard pointed across the room.

"Thanks." Martin repocketed his ID and trotted across the hall. The suit and tie were beginning to bug him a bit now. He wasn't really a suit wearing person but he didn't think the FBI would stand for jeans.

"Coming through." He dodged around a group of priests to join the end of a line of orange clad Buddhists. We worked his way along to the front of the queue. "Martin FBI." He flipped the ID at the guard on the door.

"Fine Sir, If you want to step through to the next room. We are just searching these guys. The young police guard waved him through to the next room where Willis was already waiting for him.

"Hey." Martin casually waved at him. "If I didn't know any better. I would think you were following me." He grinned and gave a little laugh. It was impossible to work out what Willis was doing as he was hidden behind his sunglasses.

The room began to fill up with searched Buddhists. Martin tapped his jacket pocket. He still had the camera that he had been given back at HQ. He only had to get off one shot but that wasn't going to be easy with eagle eyed Willis in the room. He had already moved the camera down to an outside pocket so that nobody thought he was going for a gun.

As the room filled, Willis moved across to the same side of the wall as Martin.

"Hans." Simon flicked the map up onto the screen. Hans arrived, with his chair.

"What's up?"

"He's starting to panic." Hans pulled down the microphone that usually lived above his head.

"What's wrong Martin?"

"We've got a problem." Martin's thoughts came out loud and clear on the speaker.

"You're going to have to be more specific Martin. We are just looking at lines and blobs."

"Alright, the blob to my right, in the corner of the room is an FBI agent that has been trailing me since I got here."

"Yep, we've got him." Hans tapped the blob as though Simon hadn't heard the description.

"Well basically Hans, my little buddy, if I do anything in this room I am going to be pumped full of lead."

"Can you get the shot?" Simon asked.

"Yes Simon, I can get the shot but..."

"Well look Martin, get the shot, give us a few seconds and we will get you out of there." Simon glanced across at Hans, he shrugged.

"How mate?"

"We've got the transporter locked onto you."

"I thought that wasn't working?"

"Hans has rigged it." Simon lied. He flipped his mike up, thankful that thought communication only worked one way. "Get the resus squad here. I want to know if we lose part of him on the way." Hans wheeled over to the phone. "Ok

74

Martin, let's go for it. I want a nice long count down, take the shot on zero and we will get you out."

Oh great, Martin thought as he worked his way along the wall, behind the crowd. The back door was opening and a small orange and burgundy clad man was entering. The crowd fell to their knees. The Dali Lama looked at the standing men, five FBI agents. He peered from one to the other until his eyes rested on Martin. There seemed to be a faint recognition. Back on Simon's screen the blue circle of the believability net began to fade. The lama's eyes opened wider, like two saucers of milk in the brown of his face. Martin risked a glance at Willis. He pulled the camera from his pocket and then diverted everyone's attention in the best way he could think of. He dropped to one knee and shouted.

"Gun." The FBI agents all followed suit and by the time they had calmed everybody down there were only four of them.

17

"So, you defiantly lied about your ability to salsa." Doug took Jayne's hand as they crossed the road and headed across to her apartment. The meal had finished with the suggestion of dancing and, not wanting to spoil the evening, Jayne had slightly exaggerated her ability based on the fact that she had been to a Zumba class once or twice.

"Well I had no idea you were going to be such an impresario at it." Jayne quite liked the feeling of holding someone's hand. It had obviously been part of the dancing but they had actually been doing it for most of the walk home. She momentarily thought back to her relationship with Edward and tried to remember if they had ever just held hands. She didn't think so.

"Impresario!" Doug scoffed. "I'm fairly sure that is not the right word."

"Probably not." Jayne grinned as she spun around under Doug's arm re-enacting her favourite dance move. "Are your feet ever going to recover?"

"I'm sure they will be fine." Doug slid an arm around her waist as she moved in front of him and they spun on the spot. "I can't feel them right now, but I'm sure the feeling will eventually come back." They arrived at Jayne's apartment block and the glass doors to the entrance hall slid open. "You are like a breath of fresh air." His hands, either side of her waist, held her still in front of him. "I have had a great night. I can't remember the last time I had such a good time. It has been a long time since I have been this happy." He smiled a genuine smile, reflected in his sparkling blue eyes.

"Do you want to come up for a coffee or something?" The question hung between them for a moment, in the midnight air.

"No, I'd better not." He stuffed his hands into his pockets and grinned. "I've got a meeting first thing tomorrow. Coffee will just keep me awake." He deliberately ignored the 'or something'.

"Well, we should do this again sometime." Jayne was on new territory here. She was used to men who outstayed their welcome, not ones she failed to entice back to her flat.

"Yep, sure." An air of awkwardness descended on the entrance hall.

"Will I see you again?" Jayne wasn't at all sure what to make of his answer.

"It's a small town, and there's training tomorrow." She started to turn away towards the lifts, a frown forming on her forehead. Had she said the wrong thing? Doug grabbed her trailing hand and pulled her back. "Hey, I was joking." She spun back into the dance pose they had spent most of the evening in. "I'm sorry. It was a joke. I would love to do this again, if for no other reason than someone needs to teach you to dance. How about tomorrow?"

"Ok." Jayne smiled. Doug dropped her hand and reached up to touch her cheek.

"I'll see you tomorrow." He smiled and then left through the glass doors, looking back to wave before hailing a taxi. Jayne went over to the lifts and leant on the button. Well, he had been right; you don't always get exactly what you want.

18

"No!" Doug slammed the table. "You can't do that."

"She doesn't fit in with the rest of the class. They need someone in records and so I am recommending her." Dickson addressed the last part of his sentence across the table towards Joshua.

"You can't do this." Doug pleaded directly to Joshua. "She could be an exceptional student."

"Exceptional at what?" Dickson sneered.

"One more comment like that and I am going to punch you through to next week."

"Doug." Joshua barked at him and he returned to his chair.

"With all due respect, I am the head of training." Dickson straightened his tie.

"Yes." Joshua tapped his pen on the desk. "But Doug has trained some exceptional agents in his time."

"Sir, they are the most disrespectful bunch of agents that we have. They have more reprimands between them than all of the other agents added together." Dickson was one for sticking to the book. If you can't do it properly then don't do it.

"They get the job done." Joshua tapped his pen again. "I wonder if you would leave us alone for a moment Mr Dickson." Dickson rose from his chair with a smug grin. So, the reprimand was to be in private. As the door shut, Doug sprang from his chair.

"You can't be seriously going to do this."

"Shut up and sit down." Joshua walked back to his desk. "Drink?" He took Doug's silence as acceptance. It was a bit early but Joshua was finding himself drinking more and more these days. How had Doug dealt with this stress for centuries and yet looked so fresh? "You've trained some of our best agents Doug, do you really think she has got something?"

"Have you seen the people he is turning out? Swots. They know the book from cover to cover but they have about this much initiative." Doug held up his hand, his fingers a few millimetres apart.

"Yes, very good." Joshua handed him the drink. "Has she got something?"

"I think so." Doug emphasised the first word rather than the second.

"Right, well we will just transfer her to you and you can train her, one on one." Joshua sat back, quite pleased with himself that he had come up with an idea that effectively dragged Doug back towards his old job.

"No."

"Pardon me?"

"No Josh, I can't do that." Joshua flicked through some papers on his desk as though he hadn't heard.

"Are you trying to tell me you have some emotional attachment to this girl that would affect the training?"

"Yes." Doug downed his drink and put the glass back onto the desk.

"Bollocks." Joshua looked up from the papers. "She was only assigned to training two days ago, you only met her yesterday. The most you could possibly have had is one night together. I've known you since you died Doug and you are way too shallow to form that sort of emotional dependency in one day."

"Thanks Josh."

"You are just scared. It's nearly nine months since you returned from Hell, three months since you got out of rehab. You are no use to us trapped down in that office pushing paper around Doug, we need you back up and in the field." Joshua reached behind him for the whisky bottle and topped up the two glasses. "How is the counselling going?"

"It's over." Doug reached across and took the glass.

"I've read the file Doug; I know what went on down there. We are prepared to draw a veil over how exactly we found out that we had to get you out. I have my suspicions but we will let that go. You've had six months of our best treatment. I think the best thing you can do is get back to your real job and what could absorb you more than an exceptional student all to yourself." Joshua downed his second glass, "Besides, I can't take much more of supervising Martin and Simon, how on Earth do you deal with it?" He didn't wait for a reply. "Now, is there any reason why you can not train Miss Pottage?"

"No Josh."

"Your slipping Doug, I saw you at Gino's." It had done Joshua's heart good to catch a glimpse of his colleagues' former character again.

"I just..." Doug tried to grasp the right words, "I thought temptation was best avoided just now."

"Sound idea Doug, but you didn't avoid the temptation, you just avoided the 'sin'." Joshua put the word sin into manual apostrophes. "Send Dickson in." Joshua spoke to his intercom. The door opened and Dickson appeared.

"Right Dickson, Doug is going to train Miss Pottage, he thinks she has something, so send one of your guys down to records." Dickson started to open his mouth. "That will be all thank you." Joshua looked straight at him, as though wondering why he was still there.

19

"I take it he is alright." Michael helped himself to the chair beside Joshua and surveyed the gathering group around the table.

"He got out of reconstruction this morning, they seem to think he is alright. Nothing was actually missing they just needed to pull it all together again."

"Good, good. Are they coming to this meeting?" Joshua raised a questioning eyebrow. Surely Michael did not think they should actually be in the meeting.

"They are outside if we need them but I'd be pretty desperate before I brought them in here." Joshua brushed down his trousers to create a bit of noise and leant into Michael so that he was not heard.

"I understand that." Michael gave Joshua's arm a little pat. "They aren't the easiest team to look after."

"No, we need Doug back."

"We do." Michael agreed "I understand that might be likely."

"We are working on it." Joshua felt slightly more confident about this now that he had Doug back training someone.

"Good, do we have the pictures?"

"Yes, two beauties. They might be an unorthodox team but they certainly deliver." Joshua produced the two hard copies of the photographs and slid them across to Michael.

Photography is a funny thing. Some ancient tribes believe a photograph can steal your soul, and they are not far wrong. From Martin's original picture they had developed two prints.

The first was external showing someone who appeared to be the Dali Lama. The second was a spiritual print, coloured rather like those auras that are meant to exist around people and it showed someone who was defiantly not the Dali Lama.

The room silenced as Gabriel exited the lift and made his way to the head of the table.

"Well Michael, you assured us that you had men who could sort this problem out. The clouds are getting darker day by day. What have you got for us?"

"I'm going to let Joshua explain what our preliminary ground work has discovered." Michael indicated for Joshua to take the floor. There were times when Joshua wished his boss would grab a little more of the lime light and not be so generous with acknowledging everyone's contributions. It was only the second time that Joshua had had to address the general committee.

"Our first step was to confirm the identity of this man in Washington. We sent in an agent who obtained this shot." The first photo appeared on the large slide at the top of the room as the room lights dimmed. "The man in the centre is the Dali Lama, externally at least."

"Excuse me." Gabriel raised a finger in a token gesture of politeness. "What are all those people doing?"

"I'm reliably informed, Sir, that they are in the process of getting off of their knees, whilst panicking."

"Ah, of course." Gabriel studied the photo again. "How silly of me not to have noticed."

"If we now look at the spiritual print." Joshua changed the slide. There was a murmur around the room. "It's a good disguise but you will see the man in the middle has changed. The nose is slightly longer and there is a distinctive five o'clock shadow. If we superimpose them it becomes more obvious."

There was another murmur as the two images were merged. It left a mess in the centre where they were different.

"So, it is confirmed, that is not the Dali Lama."

"It is not." Joshua returned to his seat and the lights came up.

"So, Michael, what is the rest of your plan?" Gabriel turned to face his colleague.

"I think having confirmed that the Dali Lama is not the Dali Lama we have to establish who is the Dali Lama and where he is. We need to find out who the person is who is posing as the Dali Lama and why. Records are starting on the first issue." Jenkins from monitoring nodded in confirmation,

"We have got him in London but we can only get a spiritual reading from here. We will need an external ID."

"And then what?" Gabriel steepled his fingers and pursed his lips.

"I think we need an intention reading on the imposter. We are fighting in the dark until we get that but I would say we will probably need to take some evasive action." Michael relaxed back in his chair. "I often find these things are better dealt with by the people on the ground."

"Who are you putting onto it?" Gabriel asked.

"Wilcox and Metcalfe."

"Ah." Gabriel appeared to let out a little sigh. "Who is supervising them? Is Doug back?"

"Not yet. Joshua is looking after them." There was an exchange of glances between Michael and Gabriel.

"Can you brief them fully before they go. I don't want any screw ups with this one." Gabriel tapped the edge of the table nervously. "Alright, let's move on to the next item on the agenda." He looked down the table. "Joshua, you may leave."

20

The alarm went off. It was an old-fashioned alarm with a hammer between two bells. A hand appeared from below the quilt and pushed the clock off of the bedside table.

"Get up Richard. It's eight o'clock already." The message was accompanied by hammering on the bedroom door. Eight o'clock on a Sunday morning and he had to get up. It was bad enough having to get up during the week for school, but on a Sunday too! He poked his head out from under the cover. At least it appeared to be a nice day; the sunlight was streaming in through the curtains. With one big effort, he pushed back the duvet and staggered towards the bathroom. Richard Elliot had a job at the local bakery. He was one of those conscientious young men who had realised that life as a student wasn't going to be all roses and was considerably enhanced by a lump sum of savings. Not that working in the bakery shop paid very well. Even with the small section set aside for teas and coffee, very few people left tips. He'd once been given a five pound note for returning a dog that an old lady had left tied to the leg of a table. That had more than doubled his accumulated tips for the year.

He stepped out of the shower and gave himself a quick rub down with the rough cotton towels that his mother insisted on keeping in the bathroom and then, holding it modestly around his wiry frame, he made his way back to his bedroom. It was an unusual bedroom, for a teenage boy anyway. Its walls were completely bare; no pictures of football teams, no posters of all girl rock bands. The floor was visible - in fact the whole room was impeccably tidy. But then Richard was no normal teenage boy.

The walk into Gants Hill helped to calm his racing brain. His brain seemed to race everywhere. He always felt slightly confused, not about the normal teenage things; how do you ask so and so out, are my clothes still fashionable, is my hair too greasy, is my nose too big. He was confused about life in general. His mother had been concerned at first. She had sent him to a counsellor who Richard had reduced to tears in minutes, and then to a specialist who had come to the conclusion that Richard was a bit 'special'. None of it helped in the slightest and the confusion still grew.

"Morning Mr Wiseman." He waved to the master baker as he entered the shop full of people queuing for bagels. The shop was famous for its bagels which, in a predominantly Jewish area where everybody made bagels, was a bit of a coup. You could have a bagel with anything, except bacon obviously, although smoked salmon and cream cheese was the favourite. Richard could make a mean bagel but he was not sure how this would go down at his new college, for he had found out yesterday that he had been accepted at St Luke's seminary. Yes, the bagel baker extraordinaire was a catholic, not only that but he was going to be a priest, which made rather a joke of his saving up for a riotous student life. And, as if that didn't throw the poor boy's soul into enough torment he was, of course, the Dali Lama.

21

Martin ducked under the surface and tumble turned. He struck out for the far end again. The pool was great; neither too cold nor too warm and his solitude meant no added turbulence. He saw the feet at the end of the pool side when he was still ten metres out.

"Martin." Joshua crouched down as the swimmer approached. "Could I have a word?"

Martin stood up, ran his hands back over his short brown hair and pinched the remaining water from his nose.

"Is it going to take long?"

"Don't get stroppy Martin. I have had a whole day of people being stroppy." The memo from Dickson still sat on Joshua's desk. He had secretly hoped it would be a resignation, but no such luck it was just a memo complaining about the reassignment of students. Who sent memos anyway! The man was stuck in the 1970's. Martin left the pool in silence and picked up the towelling robe that had been left at the side. "I want you both for a briefing. I really wanted it tonight but I can't find Simon."

"He left town after the meeting."

"Well, go and get him back. I want to see you both in my office." Joshua glanced at his watch. "If you can't make it before eight tonight then be there at eight tomorrow morning."

"I take it something is going down." Martin padded around the pool towards the changing rooms.

"Yes." Joshua seemed lost in thought for a few seconds. "How are you?"

"Oh I'm fine. It will take more than two hours lost in the atmosphere to change me." Martin grinned.

"Good. I'll get a full debrief tomorrow, eight o'clock, and don't be late." With that last command, Joshua left.

*

Jayne woke at 7.30am, she rolled over and tried to go back to sleep but she couldn't. She had spent last night thinking. It seemed like heaven was going to be an awful lot like Earth. She had never been very good at relationships down there either. She eventually gave up any hope of returning to sleep and shuffled into the kitchen to make a cup of coffee. There was a note lying on the mat, it must have been shoved under the door before she woke. She picked it up and shuffled on. As the kettle boiled, she flicked it open.

No training today - meet me at Gino's at five, Doug. She read it again.

"Bloody cheek." Jayne made the coffee. No 'please', or an 'if you are free', just a 'meet me at five'. She screwed the note up and threw it into the bin. He was obviously right about heaven; it didn't always go your way. After a quick shower, she pulled on the jeans and the sweatshirt she had died in and pulled out the city plan. A whole day to herself with nothing to do. She could go and explore the city centre and then there was that gym she had seen. She would obviously have to call into Angels HQ and tell Doug what to do with his note but that shouldn't take long, and if he didn't like it then they knew what they could do with their job. She folded the map up, pleased with the positive action planned. Of course, he was the only person that she knew in town, and he was kind of cute.

"No." She slapped her hands on her thighs and got up. "If you start off being bossed around then it will just carry on, remember David." David had been a particularly unpleasant part of Jayne's life, one she would always cast up to herself if she ever had any doubts about a man. "You've only been in town three days. There are tons of fish in the sea." She pulled her hair back into a pony tail, smiled at herself in the mirror and then let her hair down again. Today she wanted to look reckless.

22

"Doug's office please." Jayne found herself once again in the impressive hall of Angels HQ, slightly intimidated by the fact that she didn't know his surname. She had spent the first half of the morning looking around the city centre. At eleven she had had a wickedly good cream cake and coffee and then she had gone swimming. She stood before the receptionist smelling of chlorine with damp ends to her hair.

"His office is currently on the seventh floor, you will have to take the extreme right hand lift up to the fifth floor and then change. There is no direct lift to the seventh floor." The receptionist peered over her glasses at Jayne.

"Thank you." Jayne turned, sending a spray of water droplets over the reception and padded off towards the lifts. Was there only one person in the building called Doug or had the receptionist guessed who Jayne meant?

The doors opened on the seventh floor as Jayne muttered slowly to herself. She was trying to rehearse what she was going to say. The floor receptionist looked up as she left the lift.

"Can I help?"

"Doug's office?" Keep it brief, act like you are confident.

"At the end on the right." He pointed down one of the eight corridors that left the lobby. "Does he know you are coming?"

"Oh, I expect he will have guessed." She half muttered as she stalked off down the corridor.

Jayne found the door and threw it open with a great burst of confidence that flew straight out of the window. She had been expecting a little room with a desk, maybe an angle poised lamp, but she was faced with a waiting room which contained a very glamorous secretary and a glass panel looking into an unbelievably busy office.

"Can I help you?" The secretary looked up from her computer terminal. Her feathers ruffled but poised for action.

"I'm here to see Doug."

"And you are?"

"Jayne Pottage."

"I don't see you on the list. Do you have an appointment?"

"What?" Jayne had wandered over to the glass panel. There were so many people in there, all running around with piles of paper. "No, I've just come to cancel an appointment for this evening."

"Ah, can I take the details." The secretary pulled out paper and pencil.

"What are they doing?" Jayne gestured to the busy room.

"Processing requests, it's a very large department. Now can I take down the details." The secretary sat with the pencil poised.

"Can't I see him?"

"Not without an appointment." The secretary gave a smug smile. Jayne wondered why the secretary was so protective. Doug must be some big shot and yet he had seemed so normal. Was 'down to Earth' an appropriate phrase to use?

"Is he in there?" Jayne pointed to an unmarked door.

"You can't go in there." The secretary was surprisingly quick on her feet. She was up and between Jayne and the door before she had finished her sentence.

"Well call him, get him up on that thing." She pointed to the intercom on the secretary's desk. "Tell him to stuff his appointment for tonight,". The secretary glared at Jayne. She didn't want a commotion in her office. "Do it please, or I'll stay here forever."

"Sir." The secretary reached across to the intercom. "I have a Jayne Pottage here breaking the appointment for tonight."

"On the phone or in the office?"

"In the office Sir." The secretary lowered her voice. "She is causing a bit of a scene." She muttered.

"Alright." The door clicked open and Doug stood in the doorway. His hair was standing up as though he had been running his hands through it. His tie has hanging around his neck like a medal, the top two shirt buttons undone. Here was a man who looked harassed. "Jayne, do come in." He stepped back to allow her into the inner office, pacified the secretary and followed her in. "So, you can't make tonight." He returned to his chair behind the paper ridden desk.

"No, I can't."

"I could rearrange the time if you like." Doug shuffled a few papers but kept his eyes on the desk. "Or I could rewrite the note because that is what is really pissing you off, isn't it?" He didn't even look up at that. There was silence. "I put that note under your door this morning after a meeting with Dickson and Joshua. Your circumstances have changed. You are now my trainee. I wrote that note to my trainee. I realised as soon as I pushed it under your door that those were not the circumstances under which we parted last night. I'm sorry, now sit down." He glanced up as he moved a pile of papers to one side.

"Joshua as in Jericho?"

"What?" He stared blankly at her as his mind raced back through history. "That was a very long time ago but yes, as in Jericho."

"So why did my circumstances change?" Jayne dumped her bag in the seat that he had indicated for her to sit on.

"Records were one trainee short, we were one over so Dickson was going to transfer you." Doug took a slurp from a mug that was standing amongst the papers.

"So now I'm yours." Doug seemed to cringe a little from the possessive grammar.

"I persuaded Joshua that you might have something, as an agent." Doug slid the pen behind his ear and glanced at his watch.

"So, it's just business as normal?"

"It is business as normal." Doug carried a pile of papers over to the door. "Gloria, file these please." He handed them over to the secretary and returned to his desk. "Whether it's just business is open to discussion, I think." He gave a small smile. He knew it wasn't a good idea to mix business and pleasure but last night he had felt so good and it was a long time since he had felt like that. He didn't want to lose the opportunity to feel like that again over some technicality.

"Maybe I over reacted. I have bad experiences of being bossed around." Jayne gave him a weak smile.

"It wasn't my intention to boss you around. I wasn't ecstatic at the suggestion of the plan and it probably came across in the note." He continued as she pulled a questioning face. "You've already managed to spill coffee over me, keep me waiting half an hour, called me old, trampled my feet, and stormed into my office. Those are the things that are going to make you a good trainee but I can do without so much excitement right now." He pulled his jacket on and slid the tie up to his collar. "Will you do me a favour?"

"What?"

"Will you come for lunch." He glanced at his watch again.

"Sure that won't be too exciting for you."

"To be honest I want you there as a deterrent. I've got a lunch date with an old friend and if I turn up alone I've a feeling he is going to ask me a load of questions about my personal life that I don't want to answer right now. That, and I would like to have lunch with you." He looked across with a pleading face. "Honestly, I can handle lunch." He grinned again and her resolve disappeared out of the window along with her prepared speech.

23

Nero's was a salad bar. A very glorious, lavish salad bar. The waiters were decked out in togas and laurels, just to look the part Jayne assumed, although it did cross her mind that they might actually be ancient Romans. Doug and Jayne were led through the main restaurant to a balcony behind. It over looked a very decorative garden full of white marble statues and fountains. The tables were wrought iron painted white with a small linen table cloth. The whole set up looked very fresh and welcoming.

"Doug." The young man got to his feet as they approached. He was suited but didn't look comfortable. He had short dark hair that was slightly wavy and greying with a relaxed smile. A cigarette hung between the fingers of his left hand. They shook hands.

"This is Jayne, a trainee." They waited as an extra place was laid at the table.

"Ah, right." As if that explained everything.

"This is Simon Metcalfe, one of the best agents we've got."

"Oh please." Simon shook Jayne's hand. "Trainee what?"

"Junior manager." Jayne slid into her seat.

"What?"

"Same as you Simon. Dickson just renamed everything. How he became head of training I will never know." Doug took off his jacket and hung it over the back of his chair.

"I believe the other candidate went off to some exotic location on a ludicrous assignment." Simon took a sip from his water.

"Really!" Doug took a bread stick from the central array and snapped it into two, his gaze boring into Simon. The bread breaking almost a threat.

"So, you're not an angel then, pity." Simon smiled sweetly at the smouldering Doug and turned his attention to Jayne.

"Pity?" Jayne queried.

"Well, were getting short. I don't think we have had any so far this year." Simon looked to Doug for confirmation but received none. "There was talk of slackening the entrance requirements."

"They have done it." Doug twiddled the bread stick in the air.

"What are they now?"

"Well it used to be the 15:13 clause; that you had to willingly lay down your life for another but they have removed the word willingly so now people who weren't planning to do it, or didn't intend to die qualify too." Simon summoned a waiter as Doug explained. "And of course, you don't have to do it. Each year you get offered the option of leaving the service."

"Why don't you send down some of the junior management team?"

"Would that it were that easy." Simon pointed to something on the menu. "Can we have one of those to share and another bottle of this." He tapped the bottle on the table. "Only Angels can exist in any meaningful way down on Earth. We just go down as projections."

"Excuse me." Jayne went to leave the table as the waiter appeared with a bottle. She felt the pressure of a hand on her leg under the table and turned to look at Doug. "I'm just going to the toilet. I'll be back in a second." She excused herself and the two men watched her weave her way between the tables.

"Trainee eh?" Simon poured out three glasses. "When did you start training again?"

"I didn't get a lot of choice. It a long story." Doug picked up his glass and took a mouthful. He relaxed back on the chair, extended his legs and crossed his ankles.

"It will do you good to get back into the job you ought to be doing. Pushing bits a paper around just isn't you. Besides," Simon sat back as the food was placed into the middle of the table. "I'm not sure how long it is going to be until Joshua and Martin really fall out. We could do with you back."

"There is a big difference between training one person and coming back to you two."

"Ok look, I'm just going to be blunt about this." Simon spied Jayne starting to make her way across the balcony so knew his time was limited. "We all screwed up. The Milson case should not have finished the way it did but the two of you should have addressed that there and then. You running off to Hell just meant that festered. We risked a lot coming down there to get you back and although I know you didn't appreciate it at the time, Martin did what had to be done. He should have come and seen you when you were in rehab but he assumed you wouldn't want to see him and he left it so long it then became awkward. You've been out for 3 months. He hasn't contacted you but you haven't contacted him either. I know it was a big deal but we have to get over it." Simon finished his little speech and noticed that Doug was watching Jayne, not looking at him. "And her hair is not auburn." Doug's eyes moved across to him.

"You are right, on both counts." He pushed the salad bowl towards Jayne as she sat back down.

"So, were you trained by him?" Jayne nodded towards Doug.

"I was." Simon nodded.

"What's he like as a trainer then?"

"Oh, he used to be good." Simon's gaze remained on Doug even though he addressed Jayne. "He used to be really good."

24

Joshua stood at the window of his office facing the park outside. He watched as the two people appeared the other side of the grassed area. One was strolling along, hands in pockets whist the other one was obviously trying to urge his friend on, to quicken the pace. It was five to eight in the morning, they were going to be late for their meeting with Joshua and one of them clearly didn't give a damn. Joshua poured himself a cup of coffee from the jug in the centre of the table and lazily dunked one of the biscuits into it. He supposed he hadn't really expected them to be on time, they never usually were. If only they weren't quite so good at their job he might have found it in his heart to discipline them in some way but they were some of the longest serving, and most productive, agents that they had. He was only supposed to be covering agent support whilst Doug was seconded to Hell. It should have been for two years and that was up in a few months time but no one seemed sure if Doug was coming back. Maybe now he had forced him to train that woman it would get him back on track and he would be able to get rid of this extra workload.

The briefing notes were sitting in the middle of the table. What a mess! Joshua had been collating the information from records and monitoring himself. Michael had been very particular about as few people as possible knowing the complete story. Not that that was surprising considering how incompetent everyone must have been for this to occur. Once the information from the various departments came together it presented an almost perfect storm scenario. At least this would be a straight forward briefing, he appreciated that about Doug's staff, no politically correct comments or diplomacy to get in the way. He smiled to himself.

"Ah gentlemen, so nice of you to come." He welcomed them as they entered the room. They both replied.

"I'm so sorry we are late." Simon started.

"Not at all, the pleasure is ours." Martin's reply came out the louder.

"If you will take a seat, we will begin." Joshua waved them to the table. Simon produced a notebook whilst Martin spun his chair around and sat astride it. It was marginally better than having his feet on the table, Joshua thought.
"Gentlemen, we have a problem."

"Too bloody right." Joshua shot Martin a warning glance. Martin knew a weird assignment when he saw one and the last one had all of the hallmarks. Weird assignments generally prefaced a bigger problem.

"Monitoring have lost the Dali Lama."

"What?" Simon stopped halfway through pouring two cups of coffee from the jug.

"They've lost the Dali Lama. They don't do constant checks anymore. They checked when he was born and ten years later and that appears to be about it. Everything appeared alright on the way to Washington but when the plane took off, the Dali Lama stayed in London."

"Was that when he was switched?" Simon scribbled furiously in his note book.

"They can't say."

"It seems to me Sir, that monitoring are a bunch of incompetent bastards."

"That's as maybe Martin, but we now have this problem to sort out." Joshua couldn't disagree with that analysis. Luckily monitoring didn't fall under his remit.

"Well," Simon tapped his pen on the pad as he thought, "surely monitoring can find the Dali Lama."

"Yes, He is in London but we don't know what he looks like."

"You need another flaming ID." Martin reached out and took a biscuit.

"Hang on." Simon punctuated the air with his biro. "If the Dali Lama is in London then do we know who is in Washington?"

"One bad bastard." Joshua raised an eyebrow at Martin's comment. "I saw his eyes Joshua, he is one bad bastard." Martin dunked his biscuit into his coffee. It fell in.

"Records are working on it but they are not quick." Joshua pushed a tea spoon across towards Martin but he picked up the coffee and drank it anyway.

"So, we find the real Dali Lama and then what? Are we talking a straight soul swap?" Simon queried the plan.

"I'm not sure it will be that easy." Joshua pulled the briefing folder over and started flicking through some of the pages. "If this person in Washington is a bad guy, as you say, I don't want to let him lose in London without knowing who he is. Secondly, I'm not sure we can soul swap with the Lama in Washington because he is in the middle of so many deities. He seems to have it well planned."

"Too well planned." Martin left his seat and wandered over to the windows. "This guy knows what he is doing."

"Yes, but who is he?" Joshua pulled the pictures out of the file and passed them to Simon.

"The only person who would try and hide as a deity would be someone who would know that a deity was safe." Simon suggested.

"No Si, that would be obvious to everyone. That's like using an ambulance as a get away car." Martin returned to the table and looked at the photos. "The more worrying thing, I think." Martin held the photo up to the light. "Is that this person might actually be in there amongst all these deities because he knows you can't soul swap." Silence descended on the group as the true meaning of Martin's comment sank in.

"That would mean he has been up here." Joshua didn't really want to consider that option but it had been lurking at the back of his mind. So many mistakes had had to align to cause this situation it was either incompetence on a grand scale or a master plan. Could they be dealing with someone who knew how the afterlife worked?

"It would mean he has been somewhere, or he is a designated immortal." Martin put the photo back on the table.

"Are you seriously saying he is a reincarnate?" Simon looked across to Martin, and then to Joshua.

"Someone seriously messed up if he is a reincarnate." Martin wandered back to the edge of the room and leant back against the full length windows. He always felt a bit daring, leaning on an invisible support. "On the other hand, this is the Dali Lama we are talking about here; the most famous reincarnate on the planet. Where better to try and hide another reincarnate. I'd bet money of the fact that he has been up here, or down there, or he is a designated immortal."

"He is not a designated immortal, that has been checked." Joshua flicked open his note book.

"With all due respect Sir, they lost the Dali Lama, make them check it again. If we are going up against the Anti Christ then I want to know." Martin flopped back into his chair.

"Ok, fair point." Joshua made a note in his note book. "But let's work on the assumption that he's not a designate."

"Well, if he isn't a designate or a reincarnate, how did he get there?" Simon took a mouthful of coffee.

"Someone put him there." Martin confirmed what they were all thinking.

"We have a worst case scenario here guys." Joshua pulled another photo out from the file.

"A big black cloud?" Simon pulled the photo over.

"It's from intentions. The last time we saw anything like that was in 2001."

"You think this person posing as the Dali Lama is going to kill people?" Simon passed the photo onto Martin who glanced at it and put it back on the table.

"It's a possibility we can't overlook." Joshua flicked open a diary. "He has a private audience with the President of the USA next week."

"Oh great." Martin drained his coffee cup, complete with biscuit sludge. "What exactly do you want us to do?"

"To be completely honest, I'm not sure." Joshua glanced down at his notes. "The first thing has to be a positive ID on the real Dali Lama. Hopefully by the time you have done that Records might have something on the man in Washington." He looked up at his guests. "Feel free to follow up any ideas you have yourselves. I'll meet with you, Simon, when we have got the ID. Go and see Hans he has got some gadgets that might help you speed things up." He turned to Martin. "If you could keep an eye on the Dali Lama once we find him that would be good. We have to assume others might be interested in him as well. Simon can act as a go between, it's just wasting time to keep bringing you back for meetings, and Hans is having a few issues with transport just now." Joshua pushed his chair away from the table. "To work then gentlemen and let's hope it is not as bad as we think."

25

"Oh, you're kidding. Let me go for a shower first." Jayne downed a little paper cup full of water.

"No way. If you had been here on time then you would have had time for a shower." Doug picked up his towel and wandered towards the door.

"Are we going to do this every morning?"

"Every morning that you train with me, we will start with an hour in the gym. Physical fitness is very important." Doug held the door open for her. "Now let's go to the canteen for breakfast."

"Are you sure I couldn't just nip home, have some breakfast there and get changed."

"We would lose too much time. Come on." Doug led the way down the corridor to the canteen.

The canteen was surprisingly busy for seven in the morning although Jayne had noticed that everything seemed to start earlier here. She took a croissant and a glass of orange juice and went to a corner table beside the window. Doug arrived with a bowl of porridge and dumped another two croissants on her plate.

"I was hoping." He craned his neck, looking around the canteen, "Hans would be here."

"What does he look like?"

"Small round German with short blond hair and red glasses, you can't really miss him. Ah." Doug dived off across the room. Well, Jayne supposed, it made a difference to Dickson's boring lectures but at least those started at a reasonable time, not six in the morning. Doug returned with a person fitting his previous description.

"Hans, this is Jayne, a new trainee." The little German extended his hand. "I was wondering if it would be possible to get down to a base this morning." Doug pulled over a spare chair for his guest.

"This morning, no." Hans took off his glasses and wiped the lenses on a paper napkin. "They are all full until lunchtime. Base 23 should be empty this afternoon, we could fit in a quick trip." Hans smiled at Jayne.

"Ok, we can cover some of the theory this morning." Doug took a mouthful of porridge.

"Theory." Hans shrugged "If you want to learn something you do the practical, not read the book." He gave Jayne another quick smile. "Shall we say 2pm."

"2pm." Doug repeated and Hans scuttled off. "Ok, change of plan." He ran his tongue thoughtfully up and down the inside of his cheek. "Ok". He rummaged in his jacket pockets and produced a set of keys. "Take this key," He slid the key he had released from the ring across the table "and meet me at 232 Grovenor street in half an hour. Just get in a taxi and say the address. It should take you about ten minutes to get there. Stay here and pretend to work for around ten minutes and then go and get a taxi. I'll get there about 15 minutes after you. The kitchen is stocked, just make yourself at home." Doug got to his feet casting a quick glance around the room which was beginning to fill up with even more people now. He laid a hand onto Jayne's forearm as she opened her mouth to speak. "I will explain all this after but for now it would be really helpful if you would just do as I ask." He gave a quick grin although it was obvious that his heart wasn't in it, turned and walked quickly out of the main entrance. Jayne stared after him for a few moments. Ok, pretend to work for ten minutes. She could do that. Some would say she had been doing that for a quite a few years in the HR department. She pulled some paper out of her gym bag, grabbed a pen and started jotting down notes.

26

The taxi dropped Jayne off at the corner of two busy streets. Number 232 was about 200 yards from the junction on the right hand side. The door was right up against the pavement, a smooth dark wooden door with no other decoration than the number, in the middle at about face height. She slid the key into the lock and with a click the door swung open allowing her access to a cool stone interior.

The house was breath taking, there was no other way to describe it. Cool stone surfaces everywhere. She could imagine the floors would make that sophisticated clicking sound as you walked across them in your shoes, if only she weren't in her gym gear. The door to her right took her into a kitchen area which was currently lurking in the shadows of the interior as the sunlight swept halfway across the large joining living area. It just seemed magical, totally unexpected from the non-descript front door. The windows caught her eye and for a moment she tried to figure out where the view was coming from as she hadn't seen anything like it as the taxi had approached here. The patio doors opened up onto a large stone surface, it must be some form of balcony with an uninterrupted view, across rolling fields a fair distance below her, to the sea. There was a gentle breeze, the warm sun. If she didn't know any better, Jayne could believe that she was back on her summer holiday. She glanced at her watch. Doug said he would be fifteen minutes behind her and she had actually got there quicker than he had said so she maybe had a good twenty minutes before he appeared. If she had brought a change of clothes, she might have gone and found the bathroom. She kicked off her shoes, lifted her damp t shirt over her head and slumped into one of the chairs on the balcony, resting her feet up on the stone edge. She would just take a minute and soak up a few rays.

*

"I must admit," the voice made Jayne jump out of the dose that she had been enjoying, "when I said make yourself at home I had envisaged you making a cup of coffee or something, not stripping off in the garden." She grabbed the t shirt that was down beside the chair and pulled it on over the sports bra.

"It looked so good, I couldn't resist." She sat up and spun around to look into the darker interior of the house.

"It is great isn't it." Doug pushed his hands into his pockets and stared out over the fields to the sea. "It's my little hiding place."

"I don't understand how it works. That looks like the sea and yet I didn't see any coast line coming up here in the taxi." Jayne padded into the house after him, carrying her trainers. She slid into the chair indicated at the table.

"This is Heaven on Earth."

"What do you mean?"

"I mean, we came in that door," he pointed to the front door they had both used. "Out there is heaven." He then pointed to the balcony "that is Earth. The door is a portal to my apartment on Earth." Jayne glanced between the door and the balcony several times. That explained so much.

"Is there a door to Earth?"

"There is, "Doug pulled up a chair to sit opposite, "but you are not going through it."

"Why not?"

"Well, that is what we are here to discuss." Doug pulled out a pile of papers from a case he had brought in with him. "Hans can get us down to a safe house this afternoon so we have this morning to run through all the theory."

"Are you an angel?" Jayne sat back and looked across the table at Doug. He didn't look a lot like what she imagined an angel would be but maybe he was. Let's face it, nothing had been what she would have expected since she died so maybe Angels were suit wearing managers now.

"Well, that is as good a starting point as any. The answer is yes and no. True angels are completely spiritual beings brought into existence by the will of God who act as his messengers. When we got to the point of needing to interact with people down on Earth..."

"Why did you need to interact? Is that Devine intervention?" Jayne hadn't been looking forward to a morning of theory. She had assumed it would be mainly physics and other science stuff. If it was going to be about the fundamentals of existence maybe it wouldn't be so bad.

"We had to interact in a more direct manner because the other side started doing it." Doug flicked through some of the papers and then decided that he might actually just ad lib. He never had been one for sticking to the script anyway.

"The other side? Oh, my God, you mean Hell exists as well?"

"You can't have one without the other." Doug was always amused when he had to explain everything to a newcomer. It always struck him as strange that people were quite happy to believe there was a heaven whilst wanting to deny the other side of the coin completely. It had been some time since we had spoken to someone who had just arrived and he was going to enjoy it. "When we got to that point of interaction Angels were actually pretty useless at it. Imagine a management consultant who has never managed. Angels advising on how humans interact was absolutely rubbish and created more issues than it was solving so, Michael, who is in charge of the angels, decided that we should form a group of people who would be prepared to go back down to Earth with angel like abilities and help out. He set criteria for selection, the 15:13 clause mentioned yesterday; you had to lay down your life for another, and then those people were offered the chance to volunteer to become the new form of angels. We are running a bit low at the moment as Simon pointed out yesterday."

"How many angels are down on Earth?" Jayne had always considered her aunt Rosie to be like her guardian angel. Wouldn't it be great if it turned out that she actually was?

"A conservative estimate is that around ten percent of the Earth's population is angelic with a slightly larger demonic proportion."

"What!" Jayne sat back, shocked. Statistics hadn't really been her best subject at school but even she knew that that meant the probability of her having interacted with an angel or a demon during her life time must be quite high. "Are you telling me that less than eighty percent of the Earth's population is actually human?"

"Yeah, a good bit less than eighty percent, we make up the rest."

"So, you are an angel?" Jayne leant across the table, her chin on her hands, staring at Doug.

"Yes." He looked across at her, slightly amused that she was so engrossed.

"Can I see your wings?"

"What?"

"Can I see your wings?"

"That's a bit weird isn't it?" Doug searched her face for some sign that she was joking. He couldn't find any so he sat back on his chair and rested the bottom of his face in his hand, studying her further.

"I don't think so. This is all new to me. You have just told me your an angel, I'm asking to see your wings."

"No, it's definitely weird." Doug sat forward to rest his arms on the table. He was in two minds as to where to take this conversation.

"Is it? Why?"

"Well." Doug got to his feet. "You've just asked me to show you a piece of my anatomy that is usually under wraps. That's weird."

"I'm sorry. I wasn't thinking of it like that. I was thinking it was external, I'm sorry I didn't mean to offend you." Flustered, Jayne sat back in her chair and tried to busy herself looking at some of the papers that Doug had placed on the table.

"Nobody asks to see internal anatomy Jayne, that would be really weird. This is just," He paused searching for the words, "slightly weird."

"Well, let's just move on." Jayne glanced up at him. He was still standing, he had pulled his shirt out of his trousers and unbuttoned the first few buttons. "What are you doing?"

"You wanted to see them." He pulled his shirt off over his head and threw it down into his vacant chair. "Ready?" His body was pretty much like Jayne had dreamt it was last night, each muscle visible but with soft rounded edges. There was a tattoo on the top of his left shoulder, a cross with slightly splayed out ends.

Jayne just nodded dumbly. Doug took in a breath, shut his eyes and appeared to be concentrating. There was a slight flexing of the shoulders and then they were there.

Jayne didn't know what she had expected. Maybe a falling down behind the table and reappearing like one of those bad werewolf transformations in an old B movie. All she knew is one moment there was a half-naked man there and the next moment there was a set of wings behind him that reached maybe a foot over his head and stopped just short of the ground. He looked at her from under his eyebrows.

"They are beautiful." Jayne was up and around the table to get a closer look. The feathers were a soft dabbled grey and as soft to the touch as any other feathered thing she had ever stroked. She remembered the bodies of pheasants that her Dad used to bring home and how soft their chest feathers were, giving under the slightest of pressure. Doug gave a quick glance to check his position in the room and then slowly extended the wings to their full span before bringing them back in and their disappearing. He picked up the shirt and slowly undid the buttons.

"Happy?"

Jayne looked at him, clearly, he wasn't particularly happy. She walked around behind him and ran her hands over his back. It all appeared normal. He put the shirt back on, buttoned it up and slid the tie back into place.

"Thank you. I know you think that was weird but it was...stunning." Jayne returned to her seat.

"Read the first few chapters of that." He pushed a book across the table. "I'm going for a shower." Doug wasn't sure why but he felt a little grimy.

27

Jayne heard the shower start and flicked through the first few pages on the table. Her eyes flicked over to the door. Earth was on the other side. She pulled a few pages over and attempted to study them. Doug had made it very clear she wasn't going through it. Her eyes flicked down the page. Doug was in the shower. She glanced over to the door again. He would never know. She could just look out. She pushed the chair back and sat facing the door. Could she just sneak a peak outside whilst he was in the shower? She chewed her bottom lip thoughtfully. Her eyes flicked to the corridor Doug had disappeared down and back to the door. If she spent any longer thinking about it then she wouldn't have time. She got up and walked over to the door. It was a narrow door; the top half was glass with an external wrought iron gate that could be seen through the window. The key was in the lock. It turned silently. The door and its accompanying gate swung inwards and Jayne stood on the door step for a moment caught in the sunshine. It opened up onto a narrow street, opposite, about five foot away, was a high yellow coloured stone wall, the ground was yellow stone as well, more of a pedestrian route than a road. She glanced in both directions. To the left was a junction with another road. The house on the corner had a hanging basket that was spewing shades of purple and pink down the wall. Jayne had to push past a few of the lower hanging tendrils to look in to the adjoining street.

She had no idea where she was but it didn't really matter. She was back on Earth.

There was a loud noise behind her, a sort of a bark and a yell mixed together. She knew it was Doug before she turned around to see him standing in the doorway with a towel around his waist. His wet hair was pushed back from his face. His initial noise had been directed towards her, she was sure of that, but now he was engaged in a conversation with an ageing neighbour who had appeared on their doorstep. He spoke fluently in a strange language but his eyes didn't leave Jayne's. He stepped out into the road and made a motion with his free hand to indicate she should return to the safety of the kitchen table. Jayne risked a quick look up and down the adjoining street before obediently walking back to the door, smiling at the neighbour and returning to the dark cool interior of the house. She heard the key turn in the lock behind her.

28

"Here for your trip to base 23?" Hans pushed back his wheeled chair and rolled into view as Doug and Jayne entered the room. He was grinning from ear to ear; a chance to show off his transport system, although mentally he had his fingers crossed that they had ironed out the recent glitches.

"Yes, I don't think I can take any more theory." Jayne smiled sweetly at Doug but she had really had enough of talking about things. She was never really good at physics. She had grasped the basic concepts at school but trying to pass on the theory of transportation in four hours wasn't really possible and the atmosphere had become a little frosty after her foray in to the street on Earth. Hans gave a sympathetic nod.

"Base 23 is empty." He pointed to a screen that showed the room outlines. "It is in use, we are just popping in whilst they are out, so don't touch anything. I will project you down there and once you are there you will be able to interact with everything in the flat. Remember that you will be a projection, only angels are transported. If the angels have brought something into the flat from outside you might have issues with it; anything of Earthy origin you should be able to pass straight through."

"What about the floor and things?"

"You should be fine." Doug gave her a friendly pat on the back. "It's not clear cut as to what will cause issues or not. We have been adding celestial substance into things for centuries so that we can interact with it. It's really just people that are the issue and the base is empty."

"Now, take this." Hans handed her a little device. "It's communication. Just hold it for now. You should be able to hear our voices in your head. If you press this button then it will be two way communication."

"We haven't trained on this." Doug chewed his lip thoughtfully. "Just be aware it's going to send your thoughts up to this room and they will come out on this loud speaker." He turned to Hans, "Do we have one of the old mikes we can send down with her?" Hans pulled out a drawer.

"No offence Jayne but I'm not sure you are ready to have your every thought broadcast." Doug took the device from her hand and swapped it for the mike that Hans offered. "It's still two way. It's just it takes some time to control your thoughts so that you aren't broadcasting your every desire to the entire room." He pushed it into her palm with an expression that Jayne thought was probably recalling their conversations at Gino's.

"Maybe best." She agreed. "Are you not coming?"

"I'll be right here. You need to be able to do this on your own." Doug guided her over towards the booths in the corner. "Just have a quick look around and tell us when you are ready to come back. It will be easy." He opened the door for her and showed her the seat inside. It was about the size of one of those old red telephone boxes, a little seat in a cupboard essentially.

"Can I get you a cup of coffee." Jayne was about to say she would rather not drink before the projection when she realised that the booth had changed. She was standing in what appeared to be a converted church. Before her was a wooden floor that spread all the way to three large floor to ceiling windows. To her right was an area that appeared to be a sitting room, to one side of which was a staircase that climbed to a balconied area. To her left was a large dining table with six ornate chairs and a large ceiling mounted light. She assumed correctly that the kitchen area was behind her.

"Er...". Jayne turned around to be faced with a half dressed man. She assumed he was half dressed, his lower half was actually hidden below the work top. He was casually making two cups of coffee as though sweaty women in cycling shorts often appeared in his kitchen. He glanced up and grinned.

"Milk?"

"Who is she talking to?" Doug leant over Hans to study the displays.

"It should be empty, it's reading empty. Unless she presses the button we can't ask her."

"Transport me down."

"No way." Hans twiddled a few knobs. "No point risking you both, let's just wait and listen."

"You're an angel?" There was doubt in Jayne's voice.

"That's OK, it's only a cup of coffee." He pushed it across the counter to her.

"No, no I mean..."

"I know what you meant." He shot her a cheeky grin and padded across to the sitting area where the rest of his clothes were lying.

"We thought this place was going to be empty."

"We?" He pulled on a shirt and tucked it roughly into his jeans.

"I'm a trainee."

"Oh, good for you. I hate to be rude but I'm just on my way out." He indicated the door.

"That's fine." Jayne reached for the mike and pressed the button. "I'm ready to come back up." She waited. Nothing. "Hello?" She pressed it again, still nothing.

"You didn't check it before you left?" The man reached over and took the mike, pressing the button several times. "This is an ancient bit of crap." He pulled a mobile phone from his back jeans pocket and punched in a whole load of numbers.

"You've screwed up again Hans. Never mind my tag, what's wrong with your projection unit?" There was a mumble from the other end. "Well I'm just on my way out." He paused, "you are kidding! Can't she just stay here on her own? Orders! From whom?" He gave a little snort of laughter and covered up the microphone. "You never said you were training with Doug."

"Is it important?" He held out the phone.

"He wants a word." Jayne took the phone.

"Jayne, we've got a little problem this end. There seems to be a fault with the projection unit. It's going to take us a little time to fix. I want you to stay with Martin. It's very important you stay with him so that we can trace you. He probably has a spare tag somewhere in the flat, ask if you can put it on."

"Have you got a spare tag I can put on?" Martin shrugged in reply and walked over to a cabinet in the living area.

"Alright Jayne, you're going to have to go outside with Martin. Remember you have no solid contact with people. You're going to have to concentrate on appearing normal. Martin is one of the best angels we've got. He will look after you, but be careful." A tag landed on the counter in front of her and a pair of jeans and a sweatshirt landed on the floor.

"You'll be Ok." Doug confirmed in her ear. "You'll be back in time for dinner at Gino's tonight before you know it."

"I hope so." She handed the phone back to Martin who turned it off and pushed it back into his pocket.

"Come on - get changed. I'm not taking you out dressed like that."

29

Nothing seemed to be any different. Jayne was walking down the street with an angel and no one seemed to even notice, she was trying to be very careful to not bump into anyone as she didn't fancy the idea of someone walking through her. The jeans that Martin had lent her were cut for a man and so didn't really fit and the sweatshirt was massive. It's looked like it would be too big for Martin as well so she wasn't even sure where he had found it. Martin grabbed a swinging sleeve and pulled her sharply to one side as a crocodile of Japanese tourists tore by.

"Will you be careful." He hissed.

"Well pardon me. The embankment isn't exactly the best place to avoid crowds." she snapped back.

"Well I'm meeting someone on the embankment so it's kind of hard to avoid walking down it." They continued in silence for a while. "I'm going to have to order you a coffee or something when we get there. It will look really strange if you don't have anything. You'll just have to warn me when you are going to drink it and I'll help move the cup." He pulled out his phone and scrolled through the messages, double checking the meeting arrangements.

"Oh great! You don't think that might draw attention to me as well?"

"I meant I would move it telekinetically but if you want me to treat you like an invalid I can do that too." Martin couldn't help a little smile to himself. She did look a bit strange. Her hair, which was probably quite nice normally, was pulled back in a tight pony tail to hide the fact she hadn't showered since the gym which he guessed was probably first thing this morning, if he remembered Doug's training regime correctly. The sweatshirt made her look very young and small because it was so big and the jeans were hanging off her in a very unusual manner. What a way to learn about the business. He put his hand out and grabbed her arm. "This is it. Just act very lady like and don't attempt to touch anything. When you sit down just concentrate on sitting and you should be OK. Simon has been in here dozens of times and appeared to be perfectly normal.

"Oh, I met Simon the other day." Jayne thought back to the lunch.

"Have you? That's nice... and also irrelevant. Just do what I say." With that he opened the door and ushered her in.

The cafe was a very posh place. It was set back with the deep walkway of the embankment in front of it. Tables and chairs were strewn over half of this with the waiters, in those long continental white aprons, bustling about between them. The interior appeared equally continental. A big display of Danish pastries stood beside the till whilst the counter held a number of machines for making different kinds of coffee. The beans were all held behind the counter in glass boxes on a floor to ceiling rack. The smell was amazing.

"Three cappuccinos please." Martin caught a waiter as he tore by.

"Sure thing Martin, table in the corner?" Martin nodded. The American accent of the waiter somehow didn't fit into the continental surroundings. They proceeded to the corner table.

"There is someone there already." Jayne whispered back over her shoulder as they approached the table.

"Oh, blow me, and I was meant to be meeting someone too."
Martin raised his eyebrows at her and then pushed past.
"Nick, let me introduce Jayne." The man at the table turned to
greet them. Jayne gasped a little. He was incredibly good
looking, very stylish and obviously well off. The sort of man
she had never met when she had been alive. She hadn't
moved in the social circles that these sort of people occupied.
He has short black hair, a long lean face and very dark brown
eyes which seemed to smoulder,

"Delighted." He extended a hand and Martin gave a little
nod. His palm was surprisingly warm to the touch.

"So how are you?" Martin slid into the high backed bench
seat of the corner booth.

"I'm fine, keeping busy. You know how it is." The two men
continued to chat on whilst Jayne studied the stranger. He
was very well dressed. An impeccable suit, probably Italian
with a brilliant white shirt and a small, almost reserved, tie.
He had obviously shaved the night before as there was a faint
hint of a five o'clock shadow already. His most striking feature
was defiantly his eyes. A deep rich brown with an almost
orange background. She felt a sharp kick under the table. A
sideways glance was shot at Martin and when her gaze
returned the eyes were a lot closer.

"Please don't sit there staring into my eyes." The voice
purred although the eyes didn't look away.

"I'm sorry, I didn't mean to offend you." Suddenly the
wooden table top was very interesting.

"I'm not offended, you can sit and stare into my eyes all day
for all I care but, look into my eyes and I'll own you."

"Nick works for the other side." Martin explained. Jayne
gave a little shriek and threw herself back against the back of
the seat.

"Oh my God, you means he's a devil! Is that how it works? If you look into my eyes you take my soul?" She now looked anywhere other than towards his eyes.

"No," Martin lent his head onto one of his hands, exasperated. "That's a Maroon 5 lyric, and I believe they are called demons actually." There was a low chuckle from the other side of the table.

"Three cappuccinos." The waiter lowered a tray of frothy mugs onto the table and took the money that had been placed there in preparation.

"It's after ten Martin, why do you keep doing this?" Nick lifted a mug off of the tray.

"Because I know it annoys." Nick's stereotypical hate of milk based coffee beverages after mid morning was something Martin always exploited.

"Please, try not to hold it against me." Nick reached across to take Jayne's hand but she pulled it away. He grinned, a truly wicked grin. "So anyway Martin, what's going on."

"I'm not sure to be honest. I just wanted to check that you guys weren't up to anything." Martin took a mouthful of coffee, trying to suppress a chuckle at Jayne's reaction.

"You will have to be a little more specific mate, we're obviously up to something." Nick grinned across at Jayne, raising his eyebrows suggestively and watched her cringe.

"How about in Washington, America."

"I don't know. I could check and let you know." Nick pulled a phone out of his pocket and made a note to remind himself. "Did you see the game on Saturday?" the conversation drifted down a more normal route for the next hour.

"I can't believe you just did that." Jayne's silence eventually broke as they reached the stairs up to the apartment.

"Did what?" Martin had been ignoring her all the way home. He had enough problems. He didn't need the moral indignation of someone who was still wet behind the ears.

"You just consorted with a demon." She stopped on the stairs and almost shouted at him.

"Gets the job done." He unlocked the door and walked in.

"That can't be right?" Jayne followed him in. She was kind of hoping that the difference between good and evil would be a little more clearly defined in heaven. Maybe she was wrong. Maybe it was as Doug had tried to explain, all really a state of mind.

"You're not telling me that Doug has told you never to talk to the other side. That would be a bit rich considering where he spent last year." Martin took his jacket off and threw it across to the sofa.

"What?" Martin looked across at Jayne. No one could mimic confusion that well.

"He hasn't told you?" Martin let out a little laugh.

"Told me what?"

"Where do you think Doug has just returned from?"

"An assignment..." Jayne bluffed, she had no idea where Martin was going with this, nor any idea of what Doug had been up to before his office job. Hadn't Simon mentioned an assignment in some exotic location?

"An assignment to where?" Martin continued over the rest of Jayne's reply.

"I don't know." And she evidently didn't care much from the tone of her voice.

"Well, he has literally been to Hell and back, and if I were you I would analyse how close he came to staying there before I started slagging off other people about talking to demons."

"I think I know Doug..." Jayne started.

"Really?" Martin turned his back and took a few steps towards the kitchen. "When did he die?"

"1565." Martin was momentarily taken back by the fact Jayne knew that.

"I appreciate you might not have an encyclopaedic knowledge of Christian names of the 16th century but how many people do you think were around then called Doug?" He walked right up to Jayne to deliver his killer blow. "Face it, you don't even know his real name." He stalked back towards the kitchen. "Simon." The shout was addressed to the flat in general. There was a slight glow above one of the chairs at the breakfast bar and Simon appeared. "I believe you are already acquainted." Martin pointed over towards the sofa where the sulking Jayne sat. She didn't acknowledge Simons arrival. "Have they fixed the projector?"

"No, I'm using the one in my flat. It seems to be some massive issue. I don't think they are going to get it fixed soon." Simon glanced at his watch. "I was going to check in with Hans later."

"It doesn't matter anyway." Martin mumbled as he hitched himself up to sit on the breakfast counter. He produced two packets of sugar from his pocket. "I nicked these from the cafe." He flicked one of them towards Simon. The sugar bag travelled straight through him and landed on the floor beside the stool. Simon looked at the sugar bag and then back at Martin.

"So?" Martin flicked the other one towards the sofa. It struck Jayne on the side of the head.

"Hey!"

"Shit." Simon looked back at Martin.

"Why are you throwing sugar at me?"

"Throw it at Simon." Martin pointed to the agent, who was scribbling away in his note book.

"What?" Jayne picked up the little paper packet.

"Throw it at Simon." Jayne threw it towards him, it sailed through his image without him even noticing. She stood staring at the bag of sugar as it sat on the ground. "Even when they mend the projection unit you are stuck down here." Martin tried not to grin. Something inside him was slightly enjoying pointing out the increasing size of this problem. Simon turned around to look at the dumbstruck girl.

"Jayne, come over here and take a seat." He indicated the bar stool between himself and Martin. "How exactly did you die?"

"Car crash."

"You can't have died in a car crash, are you sure?" Martin reached over the counter, opened a drawer and rummaged for a packet of biscuits.

"Of course I'm sure how I died. You think I didn't notice when I died. Maybe I wasn't paying attention."

"You obviously weren't paying attention because you had a car crash." He produced a packet of chocolate fingers.

"Will you two pack it in." Simon made more notes. "Where was the car crash?"

"On the North Circular."

"The North Circular." Simon and Martin said it in unison.

"How long have you been in training?" Simon recovered first.

"This is my first real day with Doug; he called off yesterday and the day before I was with Dickson."

"That's it? 3 days." Martin ran both of his hands back through his hair. "Get Doug on the phone now."

"That's not going to help, Martin." Simon looked back at all the notes he had made. He could tell from the tone that Martin wasn't suggesting they call for a friendly chat. Although, on the plus side, he was opening lines of communication to Doug.

"I don't bloody well care if it's not going to help. It's going to make me feel better. I can't believe he would be so dumb." Martin stalked off towards the stairs.

"Records should have picked it up." Simon glanced up towards Jayne and smiled, hoping that went some way to explain Martin's outburst. "Still not to worry."

"What's the problem?"

"You appear to be an angel status which means even if they get the projector working, you will be stuck here for a bit."

"Can't they just teleport me back up?" Jayne wasn't relishing the idea of being stuck at the base with Martin. He didn't seem to particularly like the fact that she was down here. It was hard work having to stay close to someone who clearly didn't want you around.

"You're not tagged."

"Couldn't they send a tag down, or don't you have a spare here? What about this spare that they have got me wearing, Can't that get me back?"

"There is an internal part. It's not as simple as that. Monitoring you and transporting you are two different things but I'm sure they will work something out." Simon shut his notebook and smiled again. "I'll go and speak to Hans and Doug and we will get it sorted."

"It doesn't really matter if it's a mistake or not, she's down here now." Martin voice came over the balcony before his face appeared.

"How did you know?" Jayne asked, wondering if he had known all along.

"You threw yourself back against the wall and hit it when Nick..."

"You've taken her to see Nick!" Simon jumped from his stool. Now it was his turn to be angry.

"Well I wasn't to know. I thought she would be gone in a couple of hours."

"How could you be so dumb? Imagine if they find out we have an untagged angel down here." It was now Simon's turn to run his hands through his hair in despair.

"It's worse than that mate." Martin couldn't believe that Simon hadn't seen the whole picture.

"Worse?" Simon wanted to add, how could it possibly be worse but bit his lip in the presence of Jayne.

"She's an untagged angel who has met Nick. She is a trainee of Doug's with, I would suggest, some questionable emotional involvement, who is down on Earth, four days after she died and near to where she lived." Simon and Martin just stared at each other for a moment.

"Shit!" Simon picked up his bag.

"What do you mean 'questionable emotional involvement.'" Jayne didn't like the way that Martin seemed to be jumping to conclusions.

"Doug isn't training at the moment. He's come back to train you? That doesn't really fit with the pragmatic Doug that I know." Martin leant over the balcony "He's agreed to train you because he has some underlying reason. You know when he died. That's a bit of a heart to heart to have with someone who is just training you. That sort of thing doesn't crop up in conversation unless you have been talking for a time. I'm not saying it's a bad thing. I'm just saying that there is something." He pushed himself up off of the railing. "You can be emotional involved with people you hate. You." He pointed down at Jayne, "are jumping to conclusions as to which emotions I mean."

Simon deliberately didn't look at Jayne as he was fairly sure he could feel her embarrassment. "Look, these are the notes about the Dali Lama case; you will have to brief yourself. I'm going back up to records and to speak to Doug." He now turned to Jayne. "It is very important that you do not get more than twenty yards away from Martin, at any time." Jayne nodded. "Martin, can you put all the parts of your tag back on." He shouted up to the balcony.

"Doing it now." Came the reply.

"Right, I'm out of here." He pulled out a small mobile phone, pressed a few numbers and vanished.

30

"Simon, you're back. Does this mean they have fixed the projection unit?" Doug jumped up from the cafe table as Simon approached.

"No, I used my own but it's not going to help anyway."

"He hasn't lost her already?" Doug sat back down and fingered his coffee cup.

"Nope, she's still down there but she is a flaming angel." Doug stared straight back at Simon, hoping this was maybe some comment on her personality but knowing deep down that it wasn't.

"An angel?"

"She is pretty solid down there." Simon glanced around the canteen as though he was checking that they weren't being overhead. He helped himself to the seat opposite Doug.

"Oh Jesus." Doug's head sunk to the table. "How did she get through records?" He snapped back to upright. "I'm going to see Joshua. He gave me a flaming agent to train, not an angel. I bet he knew, he did it on bloody purpose." Simon reached out and clamped Doug's arm to the table. Why was everybody in this situation so convinced someone else was deliberately manipulating them?

"Let's not involve Joshua yet. Let's get the whole situation clear." He waited a moment for Doug to calm down. "Now the situation is that we have an untagged angel down on Earth. She is down there with one of the best angels that we have so she should be pretty safe. He, however, is meant to be working on a time sensitive case for Joshua; the Dali Lama thing, so he is going to have to drag her along everywhere, which is going to piss him off even more than he currently is. However, Jayne has only been dead four days and she is back down very close to where she lived, and died."

"You're kidding."

"You know I'm not kidding, you met her in arrivals for heaven's sake! How did she get into Angel training that quickly? Something is not right here." Simon checked himself, now he was seeing people manipulating the situation as well. "It gets worse." Simon tried a little grin but it didn't work so he pulled out a packet of cigarettes and lit one. "He took her to meet Nick." He mumbled past the smouldering cigarette.

"Pardon me?" Doug had heard, he just couldn't believe his ears.

"When she got stuck down there, he was on his way to meet Nick. He didn't know that she was an angel then. You can hardly blame it on him..."

"He's told her, hasn't he?" Doug held his head in both hands, tufts of hair protruding between his fingers.

"Told her?" Simon feigned innocence, badly.

"He's told her about me."

"They got into an argument and he did kind of allude to it."

"Yeah, I bet."

"Oh, come on." Simon sounded a little exasperated. "He thinks you have just dumped him with an untagged angel. He is concerned that they may try something if they found out who she is." Simon took in a lungful of smoke.

"Who she is?" Doug queried.

"Well, you know, the emotional involvement." Doug held his gaze for a moment. Was he seriously hearing this?

"We had dinner, once. Kidnapping angels went out of fashion a long time ago Simon. Besides, they wouldn't want me back." Doug drummed his fingers on the table. "So what now?"

"Well, I thought we could go and give records a bollocking and then possibly go down there and stop them fighting." Simon grinned. "We are going to need your help to hide her down there."

"I don't have a lot of options then do I?" Doug got up from the table. "I'll see if Hans can start up my system at the flat, then at least I can get up and down. It'll take me 3-4 hours to get there by traditional methods." He glanced at his watch. "Let's go and give records a roasting."

*

"Can I help you?" It was a nasal drone. The question had been asked but there was no real conviction behind it.

"Oh, I hope so." Doug and Simon took their seats opposite the head of records.

"Frankly." The man raises his gaze to meet Doug's. " I don't take kindly to having people causing a fuss in my department especially one who has arrived back in office as recently as yourself. We back onto the waiting room, as you know, and it doesn't give the right impression." Entwhiste peered out from under his bushy eyebrows. "Now, what appears to be the problem?"

Doug went to reply but Simon held up a hand to silence him. Maybe a slightly more tactful route was needed than the one they had employed in the general office.

"I wonder if you could possibly tell us about Jayne Pottage. She passed through here four days ago and was sent to Angel HQ." Entwhistle smiled at Simon and then shot a glance at Doug as if to say that this was how it was meant to be done.

"Certainly." He reached over to an intercom. "Bring the records in for Jayne Pottage." A few seconds passed before the door opened and a young man walked in with a folder. "Now, Mr Metcalfe, what would you like to know?" Entwhistle emphasise the word 'you'.

"Exactly how did she die?"

"A car accident in Aylesbury. Her steering failed and she went straight on at a bridge. Broken neck on impact with the river below. Fiesta was a complete write off."

"Those are the official files from here aren't they." Simon tried to glance down the inverted page.

"That's correct."

"I wonder if you could check what the records say that were actually entered when she passed through the waiting room."

"They will say exactly the same. We do double check things you know." Entwhistle slammed the cardboard folder shut.

"How up to date it your double checking?" Doug queried.

"Within a week. We are a bit behind at the moment..." Entwhistle showed just a trace of discomfort.

"She only died four days ago." Simon put on a pleading face.

"Humour him." Doug advised.

"Well I don't know, it's not a normal sort of request."

"You can do it for us now or we can come back in half an hour with Michael and Gabriel." Entwhistle was about to launch into an entire lecture about making threats when Simon interrupted him.

"It would be easier all around if we could keep this unofficial and say we just stumbled on any information. We are on direct orders from Gabriel and any time wasted does have to be accounted for."

"Very well." Entwhistle grudgingly gave in. "But you are wasting your time." He turned to the computer screen at the side of his desk and punched in a few numbers and letters. "Here you are, Jayne Pottage killed in a car accident."

Simon and Doug were around the desk and beside him in seconds.

"Can you get more details on the car accident?" The screen changed. "There you are." Entwhistle continued to read. "killed on the North Circular by collision with a Volvo, escort written off." Entwhislte's voice became slower and slower. "Aylesbury isn't on the North Circular is it?"

"Nope."

"Is there any way of finding out if somebody else was meant to die like that?" Simon tapped the screen.

"Sure." Entwhistle set up a search on the database and it threw out a name. "Mr Johnston. That was meant to be Mr Johnston."

"She died instead of Johnston." Doug looked across at Simon.

"That can't be right." Entwhistle typed away furiously. "That can't be right." He repeated. "That means we missed an angel. She should be angel status." He looked up at Simon. "Is she an angel?" He didn't really want to hear the answer.

"Oh yes."

Entwhistle picked up the phone.

"Get me computing in here right now." He ignored Simon and Doug as they left.

31

"You are kidding me!" Jayne sat crossed legged on the sofa, the file on the Dali Lama resting between her knees.

"Nope." Martin stepped over the back of the sofa onto the seat and handed her a bottle of beer. Now that he and got used to someone else being here he was actually quite enjoying the interaction. It was good to have someone else to bounce ideas off of.

"How can you lose the Dali Lama?" She wiped the top of the bottle and took a swig.

"Same way you miss an angel I guess." He flopped into the chair opposite.

"Are you guys sure I'm an angel? There couldn't be a mess up somewhere?"

"There is obviously a mess up somewhere but one thing is for certain, you are an angel." Martin took a mouthful of beer. "How they are going to get you back is another matter. It's unusual to have a woman angel."

"Why?" Now Jayne thought about it a lot of the pictures of angels were men.

"Angels tend to be angry young men Jayne. Take my word for it.".

"Seriously, are they mostly men?"

"In my experience." Martin shot her a glance that seemed to question whether this was a conversation that actually needed to be had. "And my experience is a century more than you so just accept that it's not gender balanced and they are mainly men and they are mainly angry."

"Why are they angry?"

"They sacrificed themselves for someone, who generally speaking, doesn't live up to their side of the deal." He could see the next question already forming in Jayne's head so he kept talking. "Imagine that you had laid your life down for someone and then they go and screw up the opportunity that you gave them. It makes you angry."

"Is that what happened to you?"

"Good grief no." Martin took a swig of beer. "I'm not angry. There are thousands of people alive on Earth today as a direct result of what I did."

"What did you do?" Jayne thought for a moment she had pushed it too far. Martin took another swig of beer and was clearly thinking about whether he wanted to reveal this story. He felt a little guilty for the accusations he had made based on her knowledge of when Doug had died. Maybe they had just had a conversation like this over a bottle of beer.

"I distracted a gunning point, allowing the rest of my company to make it across an exposed bit of land and into the next trench. Most of them left the battlefield and went on to have families, thousands of descendants by now, all trace back to the fact that those men got off that battlefield."

"There was no alternative?"

"None." Martin took another mouthful of beer. "There was maybe a faint hope I would survive when I came up with the plan but it became obvious fairly early on that that was not going to be the case."

"And why are they mainly men?"

"That's an easy one." He grinned across as her. "Women tend to come up with a solution before it gets to the ultimate sacrifice. Anyway, run over the details again will you." He waved towards the folder on her knees.

"They have traced the real Dali Lama to the east side of London. They are no further forward on who the man in Washington is, having accounted for all the people who died at the same time as the Dali Lama last time." Jayne looked up, a little puzzled. "This makes sense to you does it?" Martin continued to stare at the ceiling.

"They must have missed someone." He looked across at the puzzled Jayne. "Ok, take this pile of magazines as the mountain in Tibet where the Lama lives, I forget its name." He formed the magazines into a pile on the low coffee table between them. "Now, the Dali Lama is a designated immortal. His soul is recycled each time he dies and is placed in a child that is born in this village." Martin pointed to the ashtray that he had slid across to the magazines. "I think it might have changed a bit recently but this is the traditional explanation."

"Suppose no child is being born in that village when he dies. What happens then?" There was a pause.

"I don't know, so let's assume this is correct. The soul comes down to the ashtray."

"There must have been two babies being born." Jayne chipped in.

"Two?"

"The baby that got the real Dali Lamas soul and is now in London and the one that they thought was the Lama who is now in Washington." Jayne pushed a packet of cigarettes and a pack of cards across the table.

"Mmm." Martin positioned the packs around the ashtray. "If only it where that easy." He pulled three sweets out of the packet beside him. "See this man in Washington." He moved the cigarette packet away. "We think we have got a problem with him." He tapped his finger on top of the packet. "He is about to cause trouble. What we would normally do in this sort of circumstance is a straight soul swap. Take the real Dali Lama and put him into this bloke and swap out this soul into this bloke." He tapped the cards.

"But you can't." Jayne leant forward, hanging on his every word.

"This man." Martin switched back to the cigarettes. "Is surrounded by deities. We can't soul swap with that many deities around, and we don't really want to let him lose in London."

"Unlucky." Jayne took another swig of beer.

"Well is it, or did he plan it like that? I think this man is one bad bastard. If he planned it then he knows what effect it has on us which means he's been dead before and not had his memory wiped when he went back down." Martin rubbed his chin thoughtfully. He would need to remember to shave tomorrow.

"Is that bad?"

"Yes, that's bad. Isn't that obvious?" He accompanied his reply with a raise of his eyebrows and continued, "it appears he is out to cause trouble and that gives us another problem." He pulled the cigarettes back to the magazine pile. "Alright, we've got this village where two babies are about to be born, two bodies." He pointed to the cigarettes and the cards. "Two souls." He held up two sweets. "Now one of these souls won't be released because here." He balances another sweet on top of the magazines. "Is the Dali Lamas soul. It comes into one of these babies." He moved the sweet on to the cards. "Which leaves us with one soul, one baby, but..."

"The other soul is someone who came back and shouldn't be there."

"Precisely." Martin looked at the mess on the table. "Which means we have got a soul extra."

"Wouldn't someone have noticed that?" Jayne took another mouthful of beer.

"You would have thought so wouldn't you." Martin sagged back in to chair and extended both his legs on to the coffee table. "Maybe the baby died and the soul just came back and no one double checked." His jacket, that was hanging off of one of the dining chairs, started to beep.

"Hello." He reached in and pulled out the mobile. "Hi there Nick." He looked at Jayne and then pointed towards the small screen that was fixed to the wall beside the kitchen. Two men had just walked across it. 'Let them in.' He mouthed and pointed towards the front door. He knew Jayne would do anything rather than listen to half a conversation with Nick. They hadn't broached the subject since Simon had left but Martin could tell he wasn't completely forgiven and yet she didn't want to offend him too much because he was her source of information. Martin thought he could read people like books and luckily, he was right more often than not.

"Sure, we can meet tomorrow. Let's bring it out of town though." Martin moved the phone away from his mouth. "Somewhere to meet near Ilford?"

"Wiseman's bakery." Jayne said. "It used to do these great cakes and filled..."

"Where is it?"

"Gants Hill, you can't miss it."

"Ok Nick, Wiseman's dairy at Gants Hill, say eleven."

Jayne opened the door and Simon and Doug entered the room.

"You look like shit." Martin welcomed them. Maybe not the opening line he had been planning after months of avoiding Doug but actually it kind of fitted the last time he had seen him as well as now.

"It's been a long flight." Simon crossed to the kitchen area and perched on a bar stool.

"You've flown in?" Jayne looked from Simon to Doug. He held her gaze just long enough for people to think it a bit weird.

"We've just got the tube from the airport." He clarified, recalling her fascination with his wings.

"You should have gone to Edinburgh and used the bike."

"I wasn't sure what state it was in." Doug turned to face Martin. He wasn't sure what this moment was going to be like but actually it was like the last six months hadn't happened. The friendship was still there.

"It's immaculate mate." Martin smiled and all his fears about this meeting disappeared as well.

"It was quicker to fly in from Europe." Simon brought them back down to business.

"Nothing is fixed then?" Martin circled around to the fridge and dug out some more bottles of beer.

"No. We've got our back ups working but the main system is still down. We went and saw records. There has been a cock up, you are an angel." Simon addressed the last comment to Jayne.

"Could I have a quick word?" Doug flicked his eyes up towards the balcony, indicating he meant a word in private.

"Sure." Martin extended his arm in the universal gesture of 'lead on'.

"I'll brief you afterwards." Simon shouted after them.

"Brief her." Martin replied. "She isn't going anywhere."

32

"So," Martin threw himself on the bed and settled back with his hands behind his head, legs crossed at the ankles. "You want a quiet chat." Below, Simon turned some music on to drown out their conversation.

"Mmm." Doug stood at the end of the bed, his hands thrust in his pockets, his shoulders slouched. "I haven't really had a chance to thank you for getting me out. I know we weren't exactly on the best of terms before..."

"That's alright mate, I wasn't going to leave you down there, was I? I should have come and seen you when you were in rehab." Martin rolled up to sitting in the edge of the bed, thinking the supine gesture probably didn't match the topic of conversation.

"To be fair, you were the last person I would have wanted to see." Doug walked over to the balcony and looked down at Simon and Jayne, deep in conversation.

"I'm..., you were right in the Milson case. I was being pig headed." Martin pushed himself up off of the bed. He had run through this scenario multiple times over the last few months. It has never been this hard in his imagination. "I'm sorry."

Doug turned around and leant on the balcony, as Martin continued.

"I'm sorry I shot your wife in front of you." Martin ran his hand back through his hair and looked away. Doug let out a little sigh.

"Martin, I spent a long time in rehab but I know now, that that was not my wife."

"You didn't know that when I shot her and I shouldn't have done it in front of you." Martin still wasn't looking at Doug. "I was just so mad at what they were doing."

"How did you know?" Doug had his suspicions but he had never had the opportunity to ask how the whole rescue mission came about.

"I got a call. Someone let it slip to Nick. They thought they were going too far. Nick got us in." Martin rolled across the bed to the drawer that was at the far side. He rummaged around and produced a large brown file. "Here."

"What this?"

"It is the file on you from Hell." He handed it across.

"Shouldn't this have been part of your report?" Doug took the file but didn't flick through it.

"Probably, but you don't want that much incriminating evidence lying around. I didn't report that we lifted it." Doug reached out to take Martins hand.

"Thanks mate. I'm so sorry." Martin pulled him in and they gave each other a hug. They separated after a moment to an awkward silence. "You know that she is stuck down here don't you." Doug looked over the balcony back at Simon and Jayne.

"I had kind of guessed that. "Martin took the opportunity of Doug facing the other way to wipe his hand across his face and remove the start of a few tears. "There must be a way of getting her back up."

"I'll get a fake passport made." Doug glanced across at Martin as he joined him at the balcony. "We can take her back through my house. We're trying to keep it quiet at the moment."

"Wise move." Martin remarked. "I'm a bit concerned that they might try to use her to get back at you."

"We had dinner once Martin." Doug continued to look at the couple down in the main flat, deep in conversation over the briefing file.

"I meant because you are training her." There was a moments silence. "You protested a bit too much there mate."

"Fair enough." Doug leant his elbows on the balcony rail. He felt a bit of relief at his feelings being called out by his friend. Even after a year of silence, Martin could read him like a book. "Can you use her down here?"

"Absolutely. She's a bright spark with a big dose of attitude."

"She reminds me of when I trained you." Doug glanced across at Martin.

"I don't remember us sleeping together?" Martin pushed his luck. There was silence for a moment, had he gone too far?

"You would have remembered." Doug grinned. He had missed this interaction over the last year. "We haven't. One dinner and a very painful salsa session." Martin laughed in reply and slapped him on the back as he headed across towards the stairs. "Could you ask her to come up?"

"Are you going to tell her?" Martin paused at the top of the stairs.

"I understood from Simon that you had already said something. I can't leave her thinking that Nick and I are on a par." Martin shrugged and shot downstairs.

"Well?" Jayne appeared at the top of the stairs, hands resting in her jean pockets and her sweatshirt hanging off one shoulder.

"Have I done something to upset you?" An attitude seemed to have developed.

"I don't think you have been particularly straight with me." Her arms moved to a defensive fold across her chest.

"Sit down." Doug indicated the edge of the bed. "I take it we are referring to some of Martin's comments about Hell."

"That, and what is your name?" She walked to the edge of the bed but didn't sit down. It seemed too subservient a position.

"My name?" Doug hadn't been expecting that one.

"We go out to dinner, we go dancing and then I discover you lied to me about your name. I don't have any idea who you even are." Jayne brought her voice down to a very accusatory hiss, aware that the music downstairs had been turned down.

"My name is Jacques La Valette. I have been called Doug for over 300 years. If someone gave you this bit of information then they were just trying to needle you, and it worked." There was silence. The arms uncrossed.

"Why Doug?"

"Because I was good at digging myself out of holes." Jayne turned away and muttered something under her breath. Martin had managed to get right under her skin within the first few hours of meeting her.

"And Hell?"

"I was down in Hell as the ambassador. I admit I took the job after Martin and I had had a bit of an argument over a previous case. I got tricked in to doing some things down there that I am not proud of. Martin and Simon came down and rescued me. They put their lives on the line for me. It was particularly violent and it's taken me six months of counselling to get back to work. This is the first time Martin and I have really seen each other for over a year. If this is going to cause a problem then say and we can terminate your training now." He walked over to her and took hold of her shoulders, turning her to face him. "Look into my eyes Jayne. Do I bear any resemblance to Nick?" She looked at the two blue mill ponds in front of her and felt his breath on her face.

"No." It was little more than a murmur.

"Now, you are stuck down here for the moment so you are going to get a little on the job training. I know Martin can be a little unorthodox but he is one of our best."

"Did you train him?" It was a genuine question rather than a snide comment.

"Yes, I did. We worked together for a time and then he set off on his own with Simon." Doug released her shoulders and now she sat down on the bed.

"How can he work with a demon? I was struggling enough with their being a heaven and angels and everything and then to find that they work with the other side as well it all seems so..." She was lost for the words to explain it.

"Give Nick a bit of slack Jayne. It was him who told Martin that they needed to get me out of Hell. We have had a lot of good tips from him in the past. Just remember what he is, always remember that what he says may not be true and don't get attached."

"What happened to you in Hell?" The question hung in the silence between them. Doug held her gaze. Was he contemplating telling her? Did she really want to know? He took a deep breath.

"I will tell you, when this is all over." He tried a little grin but his eyes had lost their sparkle. " I would go and buy some clothes if I were you." He produced a wallet from his back pocket and handed her a pile of notes. "Whatever fits best but I would lay off the little black dresses, especially in front of Martin."

"They're alright in front of you, but not Martin?" Jayne picked up the money and shoved it into her pocket as she got up off of the bed.

"They are fine in front of me." Some of the sparkle returned. "I wouldn't suggest it in front of Martin, and defiantly not Nick."

"Right." Martin watched them as they descended the stairs to join them. They seemed happy enough, no obvious wounds and he hadn't heard any shouting. "We have a list of things we want you to check." He quite liked the fact that they were all in one room again and talking about a case. It was almost like he could forget the last year had actually happened. "Check up on a spare soul."

"A spare soul?" Simon scribbled it into his notebook.

"We are working on the theory that the man in Washington is a soul that has bypassed the normal channels. This means that the soul that was destined for his body would have been extra at the time." Jayne had swung into the kitchen on her return from upstairs and now deposited a fresh selection of beer bottles into the middle of the coffee table.

"By passed the normal route?" Doug took a bottle. "Meaning he is straight from Hell?"

"That's the theory I'm working on. He certainly looks like one mean bastard." Martin pulled a bottle over.

"You've seen him?"

"That was our first job." Simon flicked back a few pages in his notebook. "He reads on the monitors as normal so we had to get an external ID to prove that it was the Dali Lamas body."

"And the soul of the Lama?"

"He is in Ilford somewhere. Which brings us to this." Simon reached into his shirt pocket and produced a small plastic wallet. "I had the boys in monitoring knock this up quickly." He held it out for the others to see." It's a mobile soul detection kit. This card slots into the front of the wallet like

154

this. It's a pink colour at the moment but if it is exposed to the soul of the Dali Lama, it will turn black." He threw it across to Martin. "There is a pack of spare cards too."

"What sort of range are we talking?" Martin turned it over a few times in his hand before slipping it into his jeans pocket.

"About one and a half metres." They set it close so that you wouldn't be confused by passers by or crowds."

"Good." Martin picked up his beer again. "Now, we are going to Wiseman's bakery tomorrow. I've got Nick doing a bit of digging for me. What is the plan with Jayne?"

"What is the chance of you knowing someone at Wiseman's?" Doug asked.

"Pretty slim."

"Hans is producing a fake passport but it's taking him time and the transporters are his top priority. I would rather she stayed with you. If she is within twenty foot of one of us whilst she is out and about then the monitors won't pick her up." He turned to Jayne. "If you meet anyone you know then you will just have to deny it. Is there anything you can do to change your appearance? Something with your hair, or dress differently?" Doug ran out of suggestions.

"I'll go and buy some clothes." Jayne drained her bottle. "Can I go out on my own?" She knew the answer.

"I would rather you didn't." Doug glanced across at Martin.

"On your bike mate. I am not going clothes shopping. I'll stay here and get rebriefed. If you are that concerned about it, you go."

33

"How about this one?" Jayne stepped out of the changing room and spun around.

"Looks great." Doug sat on the chair opposite. He was leaning forward, his elbows on his knees, looking in the other direction.

"Doug." The whine sounded just like the one in the last shop but he turned around smiling anyway. "It looks wonderful Jayne."

"Right, I'll take it." She disappeared behind the curtain. Minutes later they were pushing their way through the shop again.

"Do you think you've got enough now?" They had been at it for nearly two hours. Doug had died before shopping was really a pastime. It was a new form of torture for him.

"I think so. You want to stop for a coffee or we could go back to the flat and I could cook something." Jayne knew she wasn't going to be able to produce anything like Gino's but she wasn't exactly useless in the kitchen.

*

"Back already." Martin glanced at his Mickey Mouse watch as Doug threw the shopping bags onto the sofa and gave him an exasperated look.

"I'm cooking dinner, do you want some?" Jayne asked.

"Are you any good at cooking?"

"Yes." Martin wasn't convinced.

"It's alright thanks, I'm going out later." He shouted it after Jayne as she walked off to the kitchen. "God knows what she is going to cook, there no food in there." He grinned at Doug as he collapsed on the sofa.

"I'll persuade her to go out. Have we still got that little restaurant around the corner that feeds us on credit?"

"We have." Martin got to his feet. "She's alright in the flat is she? I'm out tonight."

"It's ok, I'll be here."

"I could be really late, or possibly early tomorrow." Martin gave him a grin.

"I'll be here." Doug replied, not rising to the bait.

*

"Good meal?" Martin paced alongside Jayne as they wound their way through the underground tunnels of Gants Hill tube station. "It's just you were asleep when I got in."

"It was a nice meal." Jayne confirmed as they stopped at a junction. She looked both ways as though unsure of the direction. It was a few years since she had last frequented Gants Hill.

"He's a nice man, Doug. He's been through a lot this year."

"I understand most of it was down to you." Jayne set off down the tunnel to the right. Martin trotted after her.

"You don't have to follow every example I set." They exchanged grins as they broke into the sunlight. In the distance they saw a distinctive figure looking a little out of place in his designer suit and highly polished shoes.

"You should have gone in Nick." They shook hands.

"I would have loved to Martin but it's a tad too religious for me on my own." Nick pulled his shirt sleeves down at the cuffs of his jacket in the way that Jayne had only seen in films.

"Religious? It's a flaming bakery."

"No Martin. It's a bagel shop." Martin looked up at the front of the shop and then glanced at Jayne. Had she told him this yesterday and he just chose to ignore it?

"Is there a problem?"

"It's a bagel shop." Martin pointed to the window that was crammed full of bagels.

"Yes, I did try to tell you. Does it cause a problem?" Jayne wasn't quite sure what sort of problem could be precipitated by bagels.

"We try not to meet anywhere that has religious connections." Martin explained.

"You mean you can't go in there?" Jayne directed the question at Nick. Jayne had developed some confidence after she had a good talk to herself last night. She was stuck down here. She seemed to be involved in something really interesting, it was almost like playing at detectives. There didn't seem to be much difference between heaven and hell and she was dead anyway. She might as well enjoy herself until she woke up from the coma in a hospital bed, because this was all a dream, or a drug induced episode.

"Physically I can, but I shouldn't really."

"You're a demon, aren't you meant to do things you shouldn't really?"

"She's got a point." Martin turned back to Nick.

"Yeah, she's got a point. Oh, what the hell." The three of them disappeared into the bakery.

"I'm not sure if it's good news or not." Nick pulled back the chair and let Jayne pass to the end of the table.

"You've got something then?" Martin slid into the seat.

"I might have." Nick produced a buff folder from the dark recesses of his coat. "I found this in the archives. We lost someone forty eight years ago."

"Lost?" Jayne prompted.

"He escaped from Hell. We didn't shout about it at the time obviously , but these things happen." Nick began to look a little embarrassed.

"You lost someone." Martin pulled the folder over and began to flick through the pages.

"Don't keep on about it." Nick produced another pile of papers. "We had the spectral warriors after him for a time but he is a clever man this one." Nick tapped the top of the folder that Martin had. "He went and set up a terrorist organisation in Spain, an extremist group with the unofficial backing of the Catholic Church. Everywhere they went they stayed in some religious buildings. We couldn't touch him. He didn't seem to be doing anything out of the ordinary so we left him alone. He died eighteen years ago; the same time as your Dali Lama."

"Who mentioned the Dali Lama?" Martin shot him an enquiring look.

"It was an educated guess. You mentioned Washington so I had a quick look there. You appear to be a deity short.

"Is there anyway you can check if this bloke is the soul in Washington?" Martin flicked back a few pages.

"No, but he died and he didn't come back to us. I don't suppose he ended up with you guys. He dies on the same day as the Dali Lama was born. I haven't been able to check times but I would bet a lot of money on it being exactly the same time." Nick sat back. "Are we going to have any of these magic bagels then?" Martin pulled some money from his jacket pocket and slid it across the table towards Jayne. As she left the table, Nick slid a few pages of paper down the folder in front of Martin. "These are the minutes of yesterday's management meeting. I think you should read item 5."

"Items 5?" Martin flicked the page over and read through, muttering to himself. "Shit!" He looked up at Nick. "Are they serious?"

"Untagged angel showed up in Central Europe. It was brief but it was there. I don't know how they made the connection to Doug but they are convinced that it's a Valette trainee. I know the shit that Doug went through; there is no way he recovered from that quickly. If this trainee is one of his then they must be pretty raw. I had the job of checking the UK for untagged angels this morning. Do you know how many I found?"

"None." Martin hoped his tone would convey the confidence he was lacking.

"That's right." Nick glanced over his shoulder at Jayne. "Within the limits of our detection system, there are no untagged angels in the UK."

"What are the limits of your detection system?"

"It's pretty crap actually." Nick turned back to the table. "You're probably ok up to half a mile, which is why they have also passed the task to the spectral warriors." The spectral warriors were a throwback to the old days. Whilst their title might sound grand they were actually a bunch of desk bound individuals who chased data and found inaccuracies. At that point they doned some rather snazzy looking costumes and ride out into Earthy existence to track down their quarry. It was a bit like a cross between the Americans arresting Al Capone for tax evasion and people who wanted to dressed like characters from Star Trek.

"Why do they want her, this untagged angel." Martin corrected himself, but they both knew who they were talking about anyway.

"Be'el wants Doug back. He is absolutely livid about the fact he got away. I have never seen him so determined."

"Do they know of your involvement?" Martin folded the sheets of the minutes in half and went to slide them in to his inside jacket pocket. He paused and raised his eyebrows at Nick, checking it was OK to pocket them. Nick waved him on.

"Not yet, but they will find out." Nick shrugged. "It was only a matter of time, I suppose. At the moment Donatien is doing a fantastic job of being irate about the loss of his Tulpa programme. I think it might take a while before it even occurs to them that it was him who leaked the message to you guys. They are looking to refine the monitoring system though. Give it a few weeks and they will pick up an untagged angel, regardless of how close they are standing to a tagged one, assuming the warriors haven't found her before then." Nick sat back as Jayne lowered three plates onto the table.

"Here you are, fresh bagels. The coffees are just on the way." As she spoke a young man lowered a tray onto the other end of the table.

"They look great, but we are going to have to shoot." Martin slid out of his seat and grabbed her wrist. "Can you come back to the flat?" He directed the question at Nick.

"Sure." Nick produced a pocket knife. "Let me just go to the loo and lose my tag."

34

Joshua smashed into the wall and sent a fine spray of sweat out across the court. He let out a sigh and a knowing smile as the ball shot past him and into the back corner.

"I was hoping you had slowed down a bit." He picked himself up and crossed over to the door. His opponent, Doug, let out a little laugh.

"Fantastic way of working out tension." He gave the little rubber ball a squeeze, "I used to play every day during counselling."

"You could have said before we agreed the stakes." Joshua staggered back towards the changing rooms. Doug was one of very few in the management team that he could have a decent game with; the others were all too career minded. They would develop a limp at match point or fall over or something. Joshua knew he wasn't that good but he still needed wiping across the floor occasionally to remind him.

"So, how are you?" He pulled the soaking T shirt over his head.

"I'm fine. I needed the push to return to normal and now I've done it, I'm fine." Replied Doug. He was surprised how much he had missed the interaction with angels. It felt good to be back at his real job.

"I've got a proposition for you." Joshua, now naked, stepped into the showers that graced one end of the changing rooms.

"Not you as well." Doug threw his clothes into a pile on top of his kit bag.

"Who else has been propositioning you?" Joshua peered out from under a froth of lather. Doug just raised his eyebrows and smiled. "Well anyway." Joshua continued, "I'm working with Michael on a new plan for the department. We want you to move into a position there."

"As what?" Doug raised his voice so that Joshua could hear him as he went out of sight and Doug stripped off.

"Overall head of training." Joshua pushed his hands back over his head to squeeze out the excess water and then stepped from the shower.

"Isn't that Dickson's job?"

"Currently." Joshua padded over to his bag where his suit hung on a coat hanger. It looked immaculate. "Michael has come to the conclusion that he maybe didn't have the best options in front of him when he made that decision."

"Do I get to think about it?" Doug raised his voice as he stepped under the stream of water coming from the shower head.

"You can have until tonight when you come around for dinner. Bring someone with you, Helen gets really upset if we have odd numbers." Joshua pulled his tie up tight and flattened his collar. "You could bring your new trainee."

"Well, there could be a problem there." Doug reappeared, reached for his towel and roughly towelled himself dry. Joshua gave out a little laugh.

"I have heard that she is down on Earth. On the job training with Wilcox and Metcalfe. A bit of an unorthodox pair to pick but an interesting case." Joshua combed back his hair and then dropped the comb into his kit bag. "An important case though Doug, with a very tight time schedule. It can't be delayed because of some trainee."

"No, obviously." Doug pulled on his shirt and trousers, tightened his tie and thanked his lucky starts that Joshua wasn't completely on the ball.

"Well, I'll see you tonight, around eight." Joshua swung his bag into his shoulder.

"Josh, just as a matter of interest, how did you know that Jayne was down on Earth?" Doug tried to make it sound as casual as possible.

"Dickson told me. I don't like sneaks Doug. Think about that job and I'll see you at eight." With that Joshua left.

*

"Alright, So, you think this man in Washington could be this...". Martin glanced down at the folder "Eltordo."

"Could be, he certainly seems to fit the bill." Nick relaxed back into the sofa and studied the flat. It was the first time he had actually been invited inside in all of the years that he had worked with Martin, an indication of how much they wanted to avoid potential monitoring. "Can't you guys tell?"

Martin turned to Jayne who was perched on the back of one of the chairs. "Can you make a note of that and we can get Simon onto it."

"Of course, if it is Eltordo, then we would like him back." Nick pulled out a slim sliver case from his inside jacket pocket and took out a cigarette. He lit it slowly and offered the case across to Martin.

"I'm not sure how we are going to extract him yet. Is this his complete file?"

"Oh yes." Nicks voice had a rough edge to it.

"Are these tobacco?" Martin held up the silver case.

"Not entirely." Nick gave a wicked smile and leant forward. "If that is Eltordo then he put himself there for a purpose. He is in the middle of the big bunch of deities so neither of us can do anything about it. He is defiantly up to something."

"What if we killed the Dali Lama?" Martin suggested.

"You can't do that!" Jayne cried. It hadn't occurred to her that devine intervention might be quite so brutal.

"Why not, He is just going to get reincarnated anyway." Martin pulled the plastic wallet out of his jeans pocket. "We track his soul down with this, kill him, he gets reincarnated and everything goes back to normal."

"What is that?" Nick reached across and took the wallet.

"It's a soul detector. It changes between black and pink in the presence of the Lama." Nick looked impressed as he passed it back. Martin tossed it over to Jayne.

"Your plan won't work." Nick took another lungful of smoke. "You would just end up with another Dali Lama in Tibet whilst there is still someone else in the recognised body. What does someone have to do to get a drink around here?" Martin departed for the kitchen, taking the direct route across the sofa.

"Alright, what if we killed the body. That would free up Eltordo for you guys and..."

"You would still have the soul stuck in London." Nick took the bottle as Martin lowered it in front of him.

"We could sort that out, resuscitate the body and sort out the right souls." Martin walked around to Jayne and handed her a beer. "The wallet." he muttered under his breath. He was wasting his time. Jayne had already noticed that the shiny pink card was now as black as the proverbial ace of spades. They had been within five foot of the Dali Lama some time that morning.

"Why don't you just go back and stop this Eltordo from becoming the Dali Lama in the first place." Jayne took a swig from the bottle. The room remained silent.

"You might have something there." Martin hated to admit that Jayne had come up with the obvious answer. They weren't too keen on time travel upstairs. It was all too easy to go back a few days and change things. If you did it too often it all got very confusing, but these were surely exceptional circumstances. "We could have a word with Simon and see if he can get us permission."

"What, and then do it anyway." Nick grinned across at Martin. He knew how he worked.

"We've only got to change the time he dies by a second or so." Martin was getting enthusiastic about the idea now. A few more minutes and there would be no turning back. "If we can change that time at all then it creates a window of opportunity for the correct soul to get into the body."

"Yes." Nick drained his beer bottle, "but remember this is all part of his master plan, fifty years in the making. I don't suppose he just happened to die at the exact same time as the Dali Lama. He is going to be keeping an eye open for people changing his plans."

"For people like us." Martin grinned as he indicated himself and Nick, "but not for untagged young females." They both turned to look at Jayne.

"Oh my God. You're going to send Jayne." Nick stared at Martin in disbelief.

"Well he won't be expecting her."

"No, you can't." Nick shook his head. It wasn't often he objected to diabolical plans but this suggestion was a new level of crazy, even for Martin.

"How are you going to send me?" Jayne joined them on the sofa. The possibility of time travel was very alluring.

"There are ways around the transport system." Martin smiled broadly. "Do you think you can do it?"

"Do you realise what he is sending you into?" Nick was over coming his inner turmoil at not liking this wickedly devious plan. "This man is a Spanish terrorist. He started off in the Napoleonic wars. He probably rapes more women a day than you have had hot dinners."

"That was back in the wars Nick. We are only going back eighteen years." Martin swung his legs up onto the coffee table. "If Jayne wants to do it then she is the best shot that we have."

"So how do we get around the transportation system?" Jayne was intrigued; if there was a way to trick the transportation system then maybe there was a way to get back up to heaven.

"Well." He twiddled his empty beer bottle. "They accidentally managed to take a mortal up to heaven last year. They took up one of the angels when he wasn't expecting it and the untagged person was brought up to."

"You are winding us up." Nick's disbelief was evident all over his face.

"Wish I was mate, it was all very embarrassing."

"It was you." Jayne accused.

"No, it flaming well wasn't. It was Jerry."

"I thought he was married?" Nick had jumped to a conclusion about the details of the incident.

"He was." Martin shrugged.

"Hang on, are you saying we have to get into a compromising position to be transported?" Jayne put the last few comments together and realized what was being discussed.

"I'm saying that if an angel happens to be making love when he is transported then his partner will go too." Martin looked into his very empty beer bottle. "But don't worry, I have no intention of making love to you."

"Good, because I have no intention of letting you."

"There must be other, less emotional ways of getting around it." Martin glanced at his watch. "We will get in touch with Hans tomorrow and try it out." He took a quick look around the table at the three empty bottles. "I'll just pop out and get some more beer." He stood up and checked his wallet.

"Here, give it to me. I'll go." Jayne took the money and left.

35

"I tried to stop him Sir." Gloria stood in the doorway behind Simon.

"It's alright Gloria, I'll deal with this." Doug waited until Gloria had shut the door.

"We've got a problem." Simon blurted out.

"Oh well in that case we have got two. I've been trying to get hold of you all morning." Doug pushed a pile of papers to one side. "Joshua knows."

"What? Everything?"

"He knows that Jayne is down on Earth. He is expecting me and her for dinner tonight at eight." Doug sat back and put his hands behind his head.

"How does he know?"

"Dickson. If he knows she is down there, it's only a matter of time before he realises she is not coming back up." Doug let out a sigh. "Sometimes I could kill that twerp."

"It gets worse." Simon pulled a chair up to the side of the desk and produced a few sheets of paper from his bag. "The last minutes of the demonic management meeting, let me read you item 5." He coughed to clear his throat. "It was brought to the management's attention that an untagged agent, who we believe to be a Valette trainee, has been located in Central Europe. Every effort should be made to identify this agent and to apprehend them with a long term view of reopening discussions with Mr Valette." Simon looked up.

"It would appear Martin might have had a point." Doug tapped his biro on the desk. "I should have listened to him and brought her out."

"I'm more interested in how they know." Simon slipped the minutes back into his bag.

"She slipped out of my flat before we realised she was an angel. She would have set off the monitors then."

"Ok, but why would they think she is a trainee of yours? You haven't trained anyone in ages. Who knows you are training her?"

"You, Josh and ...Dickson." They said the last word together.

"We need to get her out." Simon stated the obvious.   "Hans seems to think a holographic passport won't work, he wants it to be a genuine paper one. His main priority is getting the transport system back up and running at the moment so the longer we can hide her down there the better, but we might have to do something soon in light of those minutes." Simon flicked back through his notes from the meeting with Hans. "He did suggest we just go and steal her actual passport."

"Let's give it another day and see if they make any progress. Push comes to shove we just move her without papers." Doug looked across at Simon. "You mentioned two problems." This situation seemed to be one long problem.

"I did. Jayne went out to get some beers at about half past one and hasn't returned." Simon tried to deliver the news with as flat a voice as possible.

"It's nearly three. Where was she going?" Doug leant forward on the desk. He ran over the previous days conversations. He was sure he had said something about not going out alone.

"The corner shop, about two minutes away."

"Oh great!" Doug sometimes wished his agents were not so head strong. "Does she know about those minutes? Does she know that they are after her?"

"No. They have searched the immediate neighbourhood." Simon looked a little lost for words. "They're going to try further afield."

"Call them back." Doug stood up and pulled his jacket from its hanger in the corner. "Go down and do a Lama briefing or something. I'll go and get Jayne. I've got a good idea as to where she will be.

36

The crematorium chapel was almost full. It was twice as high as it was wide, giving the impression of a church whilst not actually aligning with any one religion. It had long bench like seats, large candles and calming classical music. There was just one row at the back that was not completely full. It was occupied by a lone woman who sat there. She wore a pair of black leggings, black boots and a black coat, from under which peeped a red jumper. She looked drawn and upset which was natural enough at funerals but she also had an uncanny resemblance to the deceased.

"Hello." She recognised the purr of his voice before she saw his face.

"Doug." She waited as he sat beside her. Part of her brain repeated his real name each time she said Doug but she held back from actually using it. If you have been called something else for 300 years then there was probably a reason. "How did you find me?"

"Lucky guess." He lied.

"It all seems so strange." She looked around at the crowds. Obviously, she recognised most of the people that but no one seemed to recognise her.

"Of course it's strange. You're not meant to see your own funeral."

"So much has happened in the last few days. I feel more alive now that I am dead." She gave him a weak smile. "That's Julia, she's getting married next month. I was meant to be chief bridesmaid. I've probably ruined her whole big day. That's Robert, he was never much of a brother really and that is Edward, he was never much of a boyfriend."

"You never said you had a boyfriend." Doug tried not to be judgemental as he looked over at Edward. Was that the sort of person she was normally attracted to? He hated the fact that he felt a brief moment of relief at what seemed to be an obtainable target.

"Well, it doesn't really matter now does it. He's alive and I'm dead."

"He is still going around, getting sick, getting hurt, wondering what it's all about and eventually he is going to die, maybe in a great deal of pain. Who do you think is better off out of the two of you?"

"Me I suppose. It's just strange." They were silent for a moment. "Is there anyway you can find out what is going to happen to you before you die?" Jayne wasn't sure if it would help. It would certainly be comforting to know that there was something, but what if you found out you were destined for Hell? Might that effect your behaviour? It dawned on her that that was actually the whole point of religion. If only people knew it were fact and not an act of faith.

"No." Doug was very definite

"But there is always something?"

"No." Doug casually waved at someone as they looked around a few rows in front.

"What do you mean, no?" Jayne turned to face him and he caught sight of the streaks of tears down her face before she brushed them away with the back of her hand.

"You could opt for oblivion." He explained.

"And what happens there?"

"Nothing. You just sleep and every so often they go through and destroy the individual souls and you cease to exist as a separate entity." Doug looked around the people, trying to spot relatives by facial resemblance. There were a lot of people here; Jayne was clearly loved down on Earth. He had been to funerals where there were less than half a dozen people.

"That sounds terrible." Jayne gave a little shudder.

"It has its advantages. I applied to go there when I came back from Hell." Doug thought he had located the mother and father and Jayne had already pointed out the brother. He hadn't considered the possible impact on others of what he had just said.

"You applied!" Jayne's voice leapt above the expected whispered tones. A large woman in front of them turned around and scowled.

"Will you show a little more respect for the dead."

"I'm sorry ma'am, she's just a little upset." Doug put a comforting arm around the supposedly distraught Jayne.

"You applied!" Jayne whispered.

"Well, I wasn't feeling too great at the time." There was silence again and the vicar at the front started to mumble on. Jayne had met him once when she was fifteen but he spoke like her best friend. Someone one had clearly fed him some information. They got to their feet as the gathered people burst into song. The curtains behind the coffin opened and it started to roll backwards.

"There go your Earthy remains." Doug reached down and gave her hand a little squeeze. Jayne smiled weakly but her eyes were fixed in the front row where her parents were sobbing into each other's shoulders. "There is nothing you can do Jayne." She felt the arm around her shoulder and then turned into his shirt and burst into tears. She had mumbled into his shirt front several times before it dawned on her that he couldn't hear her. She raised her head slightly to find his hand behind it.

"Will you stay tonight?" The hand moved and he stared down at her. His eyes looked straight into hers, searching for something.

"Come on let's take you home." Doug started to move along the empty pew only to find she had grabbed his hand and she wasn't moving.

"Will you stay?" The large woman peered over her shoulder again.

"Jayne, this is a funeral for Christ's sake." Doug hissed, as he turned to face her, glancing over her shoulder and she knew that he had looked towards Edward.

"Stay."

"Alright, Alright. I'll stay with you tonight if that is what you want. Is that what you want?" Jayne gave a nod and a slight smile of success. "I'm going to ask you again when we aren't in a flaming funeral." Doug dragged her along the pew and towards the door. Being propositioned at a funeral was a first for him. Jayne glanced back at her parents and left. She had a plan forming in her head

37

It was that funny time in Gants Hill. The sort of quiet before the storm. That half an hour before the rush started of people returning home from jobs in the city. Richard packed up his apron and returned it to its allocated drawer. It had been a relatively quiet day; not too much excitement. He had managed to obtain a free lunch when three customers had run out leaving their bagels and coffee. They had paid for them, in fact they hadn't waited for their change, they had just disappeared.

"Goodbye Mr Wiseman." He waved at the master baker.

"Have you got any more of those study days Richard?" The baker wiped his wet hands down his apron.

"I have got a few next week Mr Wiseman. I could bring a list in tomorrow if that would help."

"That would be handy." Mr Wiseman smiled. He was fortunate to have such a willing helper. He heard horror stories from his fellow shop owners about their staff.

"I'll see you tomorrow morning then. I'll have to leave at eleven." Richard reminded him.

"That will be fine. I'll see you then." Mr Wiseman returned to his boiling pots. Richard left with a spring in his step. He was finishing a bit early today because he had an appointment with Father Derek. He wanted to discuss his forthcoming attendance at Saint Luke's, the very seminary that Father Derek had attended. He swung his rucksack up on to his shoulder and strode out for home. He had waved to Mrs

Brownstein, shouted hello to Mrs Morgan and picked up a discarded sweet wrapper for baby Kristen before Mr Koln caught him for a chat.

"I hear congratulations are in order young Richard." He leant over the top of his privet hedge that separated his front garden from the pavement.

"Thank you, Mr Koln." Richard smiled broadly. "I heard from Saint Luke's the other day."

"Well done. It's good to see some young people still care about the old values." Richard just smiled at the comment. He didn't like to complain about his peers.

"Must dash Mr Koln. I've got to go and see Father Derek." He took a step back, straight into a couple that were walking past.

"I'm so sorry." The man extended a hand to help Richard steady himself. "I wasn't paying attention."

"That's Ok. I should have looked where I was going." Richard's voice gradually became slower and slower as he looked into the man's bright blue eyes. "Do I know you?"

"I don't think so." Doug released Richard's arm.

"You look familiar."

"I was in your shop today." Jayne smiled at him.

"Ah yes, you left without eating." Richard felt a slight pang of guilt about his free lunch.

"My friend felt ill." Jayne lied.

"Are you alright?" Doug reached out to steady the boy again.

"I'm fine. I had better be off." Richard turned to Jayne. "Nice to meet you again." He shook her hand and proceeded along the pavement.

"I'm not convinced he was all there." Doug slid his hands back into his trouser pockets and they continued their saunter towards the station.

"I'm convinced he isn't all there." Jayne produced the small plastic wallet with a flourish. "Half of him is in Washington."

38

Martin eased open his bedroom door, carrying his shoes, and slid into the main room to be faced with the scene he had anticipated. Doug and Jayne were wrapped in each other and perched on the sofa. Jayne's head was laying across Doug's exposed chest, her hand disappearing out of sight around his waist, his arm around her shoulders. Martin couldn't help a smile cross his lips at what he assumed was Doug's misguided sense of chivalry that he would rather the two of them were perched precariously on the sofa than use a perfectly good bed not ten feet away in the spare room. He padded across the room, lifting a folded throw from the back of one of the chairs which he opened up and lay over the top of the two of them. Jayne opened a lazy eye and smiled a look of complete contentment which momentarily caused a stir of jealously somewhere within Martin. He replied with what he hoped was a benevolent smile. He was fairly sure that Doug's eyes were deliberately remaining shut. He gave Jayne a little wave as he passed and couldn't resist a brotherly ruffle of Doug's hair before he left the flat. By the time he returned from his run Jayne was alone.

"Good night?" Martin didn't wait for an answer. "Bloody long trip to pick up some beer."

"I got distracted." Jayne looked up from her seat on the sofa. She still looked sickeningly content.

"Right, well Nick is going to be here in thirty minutes." He explained. "I got the paperwork through Hans. I'm not sure he was really convinced but your input was great." He smiled. "I'll just go and have a shower and we will see if we can fool the transportation system."

*

"Couldn't we just make love, it would be a little less erotic." Martin stood in the middle of the room and wiped his fingers on a handkerchief. Nick raised an eyebrow but remained silent.

"This is certainly the weirdest thing I've ever done." Jayne sat uncomfortably on a stool at the breakfast bar.

"Really?" Nick turned to her. "You should have tried living before you died."

"She's making up for it now." Martin pulled Nick's attention back to him. Nick took his hand and whilst still smiling at his face he drove a knife into Martin's finger.

"You want me to put that bleeding finger in my mouth? I could catch something." Jayne hadn't liked the plan when they had first explained it.

"First, it's not bleeding, he doesn't have any blood and second he has been dead for so long he hasn't got anything to catch." Nick wiped his blade and closed the knife. "Right let's try that." Martin picked up his phone.

"Ok Hans, try moving us two foot to the left, on three. One, two, three." On three, Martin placed his finger into Jayne's mouth and the two of them moved a foot to the left.

"At last!" They had tried a number of combinations, all of which had ended up with Jayne being dumped on the floor and Martin moving one way of the other.

"Right, have you got everything?" Martin picked up the bag that he had packed for Jayne.

"I think so, and before you say it again, I understand the plan and I know what I'm meant to be doing; as little interaction as possible. Try and disrupt his dying, even a second or two will be enough. I just have one question."

"And it is?"

"There is a chance this is going to go horribly wrong isn't there?"

"Always that chance." Martin wasn't particularly reassuring.

"Then before I go, you must tell me what happened to Doug in Hell."

"You need to speak to Doug." Martin looked away.

"I can't speak to Doug, the delay will mess up the plan, you need to tell me before I go. I know you were both involved." Jayne looked from Martin to Nick.

"Christ, I can see why you remind him of me." Martin pushed his hands back through his hair. "This is almost blackmail." There was silence as Martin wondered what to do.

"Sit down." Nick pointed to the breakfast bar stools. "Much as I love to see Martin on the horns of a moral dilemma, this is wasting time. I'll tell you."

"What do you know about Doug?" Nick walked around to the kitchen and leant on the worktop.

"He was stabbed in 1565, and his name is Jacque La Valette."

"Ok. He was stabbed in the Great Siege of 1565, he died protecting his wife and child and so became an angel." Nick noticed a flutter of emotion on Jayne's face. "He didn't mention he was married? It's nearly five hundred years ago, it doesn't count."

"The following year his wife murders his son and then commits suicide." Nick continued, no emotion crossed his features.

"Angry young men." Martin added reminding her of their earlier conversation.

"Isn't that good? They could all be together." Jayne asked, knowing that wasn't the case.

"Back then if you were Catholic, and most people were, and you committed suicide then that was a one way ticket to Hell. His son was young so the soul was recycled and sent back down to Earth."

"So his wife is in Hell?" That might explain why he volunteered to go down there.

"No, after two years in Hell you can apply for oblivion and you cease to exist as a separate entity. That is what she did." Nick continued.

"I work for Donatien de Sade." There was no recognition on Jayne's face. Nick looked across at Martin for help.

"What do you call someone who gets a kick out of hurting others?" Martin prompted.

"My brother?" Jayne quipped.

"Generally." Martin looked at her. "You call them a sadist. It's named after de Sade."

"And you work for him?" She looked back at Nick, making no effort to disguise the disgust on her face.

"It's Hell, what can I say." Nick continued. "We had been working on a Tulpa system."

"A Tulpa?" Jayne had no idea what that meant.

"Good God, what has happened to the education system?" Nick directed this comment at Martin who just replied with a shrug.

"A Tulpa is something that can be brought into existence by enough people believing it. We had been doing quite well on this and had managed to get to the point where we could actually bring a person into existence and maintain them for quite some time. To cut a long story short, we were told we had to bring Doug's wife back into existence. This Tulpa was then connected up to a number of different torture locations."

"The long and short of it is that they managed to recreate his dead wife and then set it up so that any interaction with her caused untold suffering on other souls." Martin summarised.

"That is sick." Jayne concluded.

"You were the one who wanted to know what happened." Nick shrugged. "I could have told you it was sick without having to explain it all."

"At this point." Martin continued with the story, "Doug and I had had a little misunderstanding about a case that we were working on. We had had a big argument. He was the best trainer we had and they were looking to appoint a head of training. I had messed up and it wasn't the sort of publicity that he needed right then."

"That, and what you did was just plain wrong." Nick added.

"That is another story." Martin continued. "At this point, the vacancy for the ambassador to Hell appears, it's leaked to Doug that they have found his wife and he disappears. Everything goes back to normal for six or seven months. Well, maybe not normal, our agent training takes a massive nose dive and the amount of paperwork increases massively but everything carries on."

"Then." Nick picked up the story. "Donatain starts to get concerned."

"Just think about that for a moment." Martin interrupted, "the man whose name we use for this sort of shit starts to think that this is going a bit far. That gives you some idea of the sort of weird shit that was going on."

"So he gets you to tell these guys?" Jayne tried to piece it together. Presumably the message had been leaked out of Hell.

"Well not exactly because Donatain doesn't know that I have anything to do with these guys, but somehow he gets a message up to heaven. At that point Simon asks me to look into it, up until that point I did not know what was going on." Nick wanted to make quite clear that he was not involved in setting the situation up.

"We needed to get Doug out so Nick managed to sneak Simon and myself into Hell and we rescued Doug." Martin added as he rummaged through the kitchen drawer looking for something.

"By killing the Tulpa." Nick added.

"Yes, that was where it went wrong. I went in to rescue him and shot his wife in front of him." Martin didn't look up from searching the drawer.

"You are joking!" Jayne just stared at Martin with her mouth open.

"No," Martin pushed the drawer shut and looked up at Jayne and Nick. "It was a poor decision. It didn't occur to me that he didn't know that it was a Tulpa. He genuinely thought that it was his wife and I stormed into their bedroom and shot her in the head." Martin held his hands up in confession. "It was me that put him into rehab for 6 months, it was because of me that he tried to obliterate himself and I can't believe I'm about to send his sodding lover back in time." The room went silent.

"Lover?" Nick broke the silence.

"He stayed here last night.' Martin explained, "and I'm not hearing her deny it." They both turned to Jayne.

"You've only known him a few days." Once again Nick broke the silence.

"Really? I'm going to get a morality lecture from a demon?" Jayne said, indignantly, although his words had got under her skin.

"It's at times like this you should re-evaluate your choices." Martin butted in.

"No look, we can't do this." Nick took a small step back. "If this goes wrong it's going to push him over the edge."

"We have to do it." Jayne climbed down off of the bar stool. "This is our best shot. If we don't do this then that mad terrorist is going to kill the President and we are going to have a world war."

"I think that might actually be preferable to pissing off Doug." Martin mused, "again."

"Look, we've come this far. Let's just go ahead." Jayne walked over to where they had been practising. Martin grabbed Nick's wrist.

"If this goes wrong." He whispered "then I will come and find you, and anyone you care about, and send you all to oblivion before Doug does it to me. You need to help me keep her safe."

39

Doug stood in the lift and studied the carpet. Joshua hadn't been that bad about it really. Doug had phoned him last night to let him know that they wouldn't be turning up to dinner and he had seemed pleasant enough. Doug has come up with some elaborate story about new developments complete with the added touch of truth about identifying the Dali Lama's soul. He was a bit out of practice but it had sounded convincing to him. The lift stopped and he sauntered out, down the corridor towards the control room and Hans.

"Hey Doug, nice to see you." Hans waved from the balcony as he entered the darkened room.

"And you Hans." Doug replied wondering why the small German was quite so happy to see him.

"I hear there have been quite a few developments with this Lama case." Hans trotted down the stairs and back to his normal chair behind the control panels.

"Have you been speaking to Martin?"

"Had him on the phone this morning." Hans lifted his stumpy little legs up to rest on the edge of the control panel.

"He seems to think there may be some way to fool the transportation system into moving an untagged person." Doug perched on the edge of the desk and looked expectantly at Hans.

"Yes, I was telling him one time he was up here about Jerry." Hans let out a little laugh. "About a year ago we had a security scare and Dickson ordered all the angels to be recalled immediately with no notice. Jerry had been down in Denmark so when the computer told us that he had put on a lot of weight we thought nothing of it." Hans laughed again. "When he arrived up here." He pointed over to the central stage. "On the stage, not in a private booth, he was completely naked and." Hans paused, lost for words "in flagrante delicto, as it were."

"You brought up a mortal because she was making love to an angel at point of transportation?"

"Yes." Hans smiled smugly. "We are thinking something similar might work for an untagged angel."

"Shit." Doug stared across the room. "I could have brought her out last night." He muttered to himself. "When did you tell Martin about this?"

"Weeks ago." Hans swung his feet down as a light started to flash in the phone. "I assumed that was where you got the idea from." He held up his hand to stop Doug as he answered the phone.

The bastard, Doug thought, not for the first time. He knew I could have got her out and said nothing. I'm seriously going to kill him this time.

"So, isn't that where the idea came from?" Hans, having finished on the phone, wheeled himself back to be in front of Doug.

"I don't want to ask this, but what idea?" Hans' face fell.

"They moved her this morning." He confirmed Doug's worst fear.

"Where to?" Doug wasn't sure he wanted to hear the answer.

"Spain, eighteen years ago."

"I defiantly don't want to hear this." Doug ran his hands back through his hair. "You're telling me they moved an untagged angel back through time and you didn't think that was a bit strange?"

"I thought that it was bloody strange. That is why I insisted on a written order with both yours and Simon's signatures on it."

"Could I see it?" Doug followed Hans down towards the filing cabinets. "How soon can you get her back?"

"It's quite a drain on the system and it's not running properly yet. I'd want to do some tests first as well. I think the first major move might set up a recognition in the system which might affect any subsequent moves." Hans flicked through a few files and pulled out a sheet of paper. "I didn't put much weight in Simon's signature; I've seen Martin's forgeries so often I probably wouldn't recognise the real thing but I thought with you having been out of circulation for so long, your's would be a pretty safe bet." Doug took the sheet of paper and held it up to the light. It was his signature alright. The a in his second name was completely missing, just how he had signed the credit slip at the restaurant the other night. He stood staring at it for a second, denying the obvious truth to himself.

"That is your signature, is it?" Hans wasn't sounding so convinced now.

"It's my signature, but I did not sign this." Doug handed back the form. "Anything else he wants to do, you contact me personally."

"The bastard; he has stitched me up before." Hans stuffed the paper back in the file.

"You and me both mate." Doug left, in a hurry and a bad mood.

40

Martin felt the chill in the air as he bent to get the carton of milk although the chill wasn't coming from the fridge.

"Ah Doug." He spun around smiling "would you like a cup of tea?"

"Don't 'Ah Doug' me you stupid irresponsible bastard." Doug remained still, his hands forced into his pockets, his ice blue eyes focused on Martin.

"You've got a problem?" Martin slurped the milk into his mug of tea, returned it to the fridge and kicked the door shut.

"Well I don't know. Let's see, do I have a problem? It could be that some stupid prick of an angel has just sent an untagged, untrained rookie back in time to Spain."

"She wanted to go." Martin sauntered over to the sofa, fighting every nerve in his body to retaliate, "it was the best way we could think of to solve this case."

"She wasn't down here as a resource for you. She wasn't meant to be getting involved in this case. I can't believe you would betray so many trusts like this. You get Hans to over load a system he is meant to be fixing, you give him an order that has two forged signatures on it, you put an untrained angel into an incredibly hazardous position. She is stuck back there with no communication and you know the spectral warriors are after her but worst of all." Doug paused for breath, " you knew I could have got her out last night and you said nothing." Doug hadn't moved from the kitchen area as he shouted after Martin. Martin turned to glare at him, placed his mug on the table as he lost his internal fight, stepped over the sofa and returned to within a few feet of Doug, although just out of arms reach.

"Firstly, the spectral warriors are looking for a trainee of your's on Earth now. They aren't looking eighteen years ago. They know we don't use time travel so there is no safer place for her. Secondly, if Hans didn't like it then he is big enough to say no. Thirdly, he wasn't me who took the credit slip so that we could forge your signature and," Martin raised a hand to stop Doug from interrupting him "I didn't even suggest it and fourthly." He lent in conspiratorially, "she knew how to fool the transportation system last night, before you stayed the night." Martin gave a smug grin and returned to his cup of tea. "She, well and truly, used you mate."

"I don't actually mind being used in that way." Doug countered although something deep down inside of him twinged a little bit. "Have you thought about how you are going to get her back or were you just planning this as a one way trip?"

Martin sat down on the sofa and put his feet up onto the table.

"Couple of days, Hans will have the system back up and running again. We can send in a tag and bring her back."

"You didn't get the whole of the story from Hans, did you?" Doug almost felt a little sorry for the bomb shell he was about to drop on Martin.

"What do you mean?" A note of worry had crept in to Martin's voice.

"That mortal that they accidentally transported up, they tried to send her back down and they lost her in the atmosphere. The system can't be tricked to often by the same person. You have sent Jayne on a one way trip." Doug let his words sink in, "Mate."

"No, no. We will find a way around this." Martin swivelled to talk to Doug as he walked across to the door. "Doug, Doug." He shouted down the stairs as Doug left. "Shit!" A quick vault over the furniture got him to his phone on the table. He furiously punched in numbers. "Nick, Mate, I'm going to need your help."

41

Jocheim adjusted the frame and sat back and looked at the certificate. He had studied long and hard to get his MBA and it sat quite nicely beside his degree in divinity. It wasn't even arguable which qualification was the more useful in his role as the director of the monastery of Saint Sebastian. The income from the modest farm had blossomed under his management, helped by the fact that they had never used chemicals and so could describe themselves as organic and there seemed to be an army of willing youthful volunteers who would come and provide his labour for nothing more than a bed and a few vegetable based meals. The labour costs were minimal and the retail price was a premium. The decision a few years ago to open up the old sleeping quarters as a parador saw tourists stop over for an uncomfortable bed and a meagre breakfast, that were almost welcomed as a penance on their pilgrimage to the cathedral in the lower laying coastal town. They had done up a few rooms to a higher standard and had a few longer term guests who seemed happy to pay a premium for a small room in an old monastery. The friars had retreated to a set of chambers around the chapel and kept themselves to themselves. In another decade or so they would probably all be gone and the church might just take it on as an ongoing concern. He let a little smile flutter across his lips. His MBA positioned him as the ideal person to stay on and run the business. It was his anchor to stop him being relocated by the church as his fellow monks left this mortal coil.

The door to his office opened a crack and the friendly face of one of the young volunteers came around it.

"I think that is the new girl coming up the path just now."

"Oh good." Jocheim shut his lap top that showed the obscene profit that the church had made from the last quarter. "Only two days late. Let's go and greet her."

"Julie." The short man in the black robe that reminded Jayne of someone from the Matrix, walked down the path, his hand extended. Her mind raced to the fork in the path that demanded a decision.

"Yes." She stuck out her hand, amazed at how easy it was to lie and noting that this man was a member of the clergy and not a fancy dress addict.

"Only two days late." He took her hand and shook it warmly although his words were anything but. The young girl just behind him gave an apologetic grin.

"Our van broke down in the middle of nowhere. I had no way to get in touch. I'm so sorry." Jayne looked him straight in the eyes. There was a moment as he met her gaze and Jayne wondered if the clergy would be able to detect her true identity in some way.

"Not to worry, you are here now. You're not the only one who is late. We have had another no show. I'm going to get Gaby here to show you around the place." Jocheim turned on his heel as he waved at the girl behind him and started to retrace his steps towards the front door. This volunteer was a bit more presentable than the normal dread lock wearing teenager that appeared. He wondered whether he could slot her into the vacant post at the parador. It would save him employing a local kid from the village and increase his profit margin even more. "Would you mind if you weren't involved in the grape harvest?"

"Happy to help where ever I'm needed." Jayne jogged after him. He had a surprising turn of speed for one with such a small stature.

"Good." He stopped and turned. Jayne almost stumbled into him. "It's a blessing to have such helpful volunteers. Evening meal is at seven, lights out at ten and breakfast at six." He reached out and touched her arm. "God smiles on what we do here. Your work here will be your offering." He gave what Jayne would describe as a patronising smile and left them.

'You have no idea.' Jayne said to herself, smiled at Gaby and followed her into the courtyard.

"Have you come from far away?" Gaby asked Jayne in slow and deliberate English.

"London." Jayne replied.

"Oh thank God for that." A fairly strong Glaswegian accent appeared. "I've been here for months trying to make myself understood." Gaby gave a big smile. "Everyone speaks English, although I think the friars would rather we spoken Spanish, or Latin. Just not everybody speaks the same English, if you get what I mean." She ducked into a small doorway in the far wall of the courtyard and they found themselves in a large, low ceilinged room that looked like a student lounge area. "The boys dorm is off to the right." She waved a hand towards the far corner. "The girls dorm is up those stairs. We've got smaller rooms, you only have to share with two others. There is a space in my room if you want to take that."

"Sure." Jayne followed her up the stairs and along the corridor to the last room on the right. It was bright enough, looking away from the courtyard and over the open fields of the farm. She put her bag down on the empty bed.

"That's the farm, the vine yard is just around to the left. We all have breakfast at six. There is only one shower so if you want to wash you will need to get up earlier or use it in the evening. Lunch is brought out to us in the fields and then we work until six with dinner all together at seven. Sometimes there are a few jobs to do in the evening but everybody is meant to be in their rooms by ten." Gaby leant out of the open window and looked down on her fellow volunteers in the fields.

"Meant to be?" Jayne joined her.

"Well." Gaby looked over her shoulder to Jayne. "We're not angels." She gave another big smile. "Although it's tiring work. No one's really got any energy at the end of the day." She pushed herself up off of the window sill. "Come on, I'll introduce you to the others."

42

"Ah Doug." Joshua looked up from his papers as Doug entered. "Good to see you. How is it going?" He pushed himself away from the desk a little. "Looking very casual if I might say so." Joshua was used to seeing Doug in a shirt and tie. He was wearing jeans today, the old faded battered sort with a collarless shirt. It might actually have been a dress shirt that hadn't had the collar attached but it still looked casual, one might even say scruffy if one was feeling particularly harsh.

"Hi Josh." Doug flopped into the offered chair. "I'm not working today, in fact." Doug wiped a hand across what Joshua correctly assumed to be an unshaven chin. "I'm not going to work again. I'm resigning."

"You're resigning?"

"Yep."

"You only took the post yesterday and now you are resigning." Joshua sat back and looked at Doug over steepled fingers. "I take it something has happened to cause this sudden change of heart."

"Yep."

"Elucidate Doug."

"My trainee is dead. If I can't keep one alive then I don't want the responsibility for any more." Doug pinched his forefinger and thumb across his eyes. Joshua wasn't sure if it was an attempt to wake himself up or if it was to wipe away tears. He was fairly sure that what sat in front of him was an emotional wreck.

"Your trainee is dead." Joshua wasn't entirely sure what to make of that. "We're all dead Doug!"

"No, very shortly my trainee will cease to exist in any form whatsoever."

"And you are quite happy to let that happen?" Joshua asked incredulously.

"No of course I'm bloody well not." Doug snapped and then leapt to his feet and began to pace the room.

"Alright." Joshua pulled out two large glasses and a bottle. "Let's go back to the beginning shall we because I feel I am missing something here." He poured out two large measures. "Let's start with 'I hand Jayne Pottage's training over to you.'" He took a sip and sat back.

"You handed Jayne over to me. The first day we didn't do anything because I had a few loose ends to tie up, well we went for lunch with Simon Metcalfe." Doug corrected himself.

"Is that relevant?"

"It could become so." Doug looked at his glass but decided to abstain until the story was complete. "The next day I think it was, I decided to start training. We did a gym session and then covered a bit of theory back at my house." Doug ignored Joshua's raised eyebrow. "In the afternoon, Hans sent her down to base 23 which should have been empty but when she got there Martin was there."

"He seems to make a habit of that." Joshua muttered. He didn't like it when angels made themselves deliberately disappear from monitoring and he had noticed that Martin did it more often than not.

"Anyway, we couldn't get her back. Hans thought there was a problem with the unit so we handed her over to Martin, who was on his way out to meet one of his contacts. A couple of hours later and the transport still isn't working so Simon goes down with a system in his flat and he comes back with the news that she is an angel."

"Jayne Pottage is an angel?" Joshua's shoulders sagged into a sigh.

"Yep, So, now we have an untagged angel down there and as if that isn't bad enough, Martin gets notification that the spectral warriors are after her. She gets dragged into this Dali Lama case, goes to her own funeral and then vanishes."

"Vanishes?"

"Martin decides that to solve the Lama case he needs an untagged angel eighteen years ago in Spain so they fool the transporting system into transporting them both back to Spain and then he leaves her there with no way of communicating and very little chance of getting back."

"Can't they just fool the system again?" Joshua was struggling with the idea that all of this had happened under his nose and he had had no idea. In fact, even though Doug was back in the office, Joshua was still responsible for Martin. He was beginning to realise the enormity of what Doug must have faced on a daily basis.

"It's only been tried once before and when they tried to transport the untagged one any distance for a second time they lost her in the atmosphere." Having now finished the story Doug took a long drink.

"What about paperwork? Hans wouldn't have transported them back in time without something in writing." Joshua knew that hoping that Martin had been limited by appropriate paperwork was forlorn.

"They forged Paul and mine signatures."

"Oh, Christ." Joshua massaged the bridge of his nose. "So you want to quit?" He glanced across at Doug. "You glossed over it but I assume somewhere along the line that you developed some form of, how shall we say, emotional attachment to Miss Pottage."

"You could say that." Doug thought about explaining to Joshua that Jayne had begged him to stay whilst at her own funeral and with the knowledge that she might be on a one way trip to oblivion but the bottom line was he had agreed to stay, and was thankful he had.

Joshua rubbed his face.

"Ah Doug- you aren't giving us much choice are you. I give you a student and within a week you have slept with her and killed her." Doug just stared at the carpet. "Don't you want to go and try and save her?"

"I would Josh if I could think of a way. I've got Hans and the lads searching back through their records to find a way around this. They have got to attempt to pull her out because at the moment there are two Jayne Pottages on Earth, they can't leave her there." Doug drained his glass. "I'm no use here so I thought I would take off."

"I'll put it down as two weeks leave. You come back here the Monday of the third week and we can talk about this again. We are going to have to tell Michael." Joshua flicked through his diary and marked the date in it. "Do you have the complete case notes?"

"No, Simon probably has them." Doug got to his feet. "Well, it's been good Josh." He held out his hand. "Thanks for looking after the boys whilst I was off. It's been a pleasure working with you."

"You'll be back." Joshua took the extended hand between both of his. "Leave the details of your whereabouts with the secretary so I can get in touch with you."

"Sure, sure." Doug broke off the handshake and gave a little wave. "See ya." Joshua waited until he heard the outer office door shut and then dived for his intercom. "Get Simon Metcalfe in here, now!"

43

"Julie, Julie." She woke to the hiss of her false name being called and looked up into the fresh face of her fellow roommate. "Are you coming?" Gaby sat back to reveal the other roommate behind her. Both were dressed in jeans and t shirts.

"Where?" Jayne was already pulling back the cover and reaching over towards her discarded clothes.

"The local bar down in the village. It's got a certain charm, and beer." Gaby and her colleague, Mel, walked over to the window and pushed it open. "You can get down the ivy at the side of the building." They disappeared over the sill and were swallowed up by the dark of the night. Part of Jayne was relieved that she wasn't actually stuck in a room with two do gooders who wanted to save the planet whilst eating vegetables and providing slave labour for organic farmers. She was glad she wasn't going to have to spend too long in the monastery.

She sat of the sill, reached around for the foliage and started to descend the plant. It was almost like someone had planted it for the purpose. It's thick trunk was bent to and fro in a way that almost provided steps. Gaby and Mel were waiting for her at the bottom.

"Thank god you're not one of those preachy dogooders." Gaby said as they fell into step across the grass at the back of the building. "I thought you didn't look like one of the normal volunteers when you arrived."

"And lucky you getting put into the paramor." Mel added, "it's lots of changing sheets but at least you aren't on your knees all day weeding." They walked on in silence for a while until they got to the edge of the village. "I'll meet you back here at midnight." Mel have Gaby a quick hug and disappeared up a track on the right into the houses.

"She goes to see one of the local farmers." Gaby explained. "They met at the edge of the fields one day. We need to go down here." Gaby pointed to a path that led down towards the main part of the village. They had walked through spaced out farm houses but as they approached the centre the houses became closer together. A few neon signs appeared, a few guest houses and hotels. "It's not quite the season yet but they get a fairly steady stream of pilgrims coming through the place. One of the friars told me that this village used to be three farms and the monastery." Gaby grinned. "Here's the bar."

It looked almost like a normal house apart from the sign in the window from one of the local beer companies. The inside was dark, not quite as dark as outside but defiantly lower lighting levels than were needed to provide an atmosphere. A television screen in the far corner showed a football match and some typically Spanish sounding music was playing in the back ground. There were maybe twenty people in the room, a few sitting in booths along the wall but most standing in or around the bar. "Grab that table." Gaby pointed, "I'll get some beers."

Several beers later, Jayne had almost forgotten that she had been sent back here on a mission and she only had a limited time in which to do it. It was a long time since she had had a nice relaxed evening in a bar with another woman.

"Oh, watch out." Gaby have her a nudge as the barman approached the table with a tray."

"Senorita." He lifted two glasses off of the tray. They were small with a pale pink juice in them. "From the senor at the bar." He indicated to a figure at the end of the bar. He had his back to them, dressed entirely in black, or it could have been the lighting, he looked fairly slim and tall.

"Pass on our thanks." Gaby took the drink. The waiter nodded in a way that Jayne thought implied that the senor would be after slightly more than thanks.

She picked up the glass, looked at the liquid and took a sip. She had had this before. She looked across the bar towards the man but he had gone. She took another mouthful. She had had this at her first dinner in heaven, that night in Gino's. Its taste was hard to describe.

"What the hell is this?" Gaby took a mouthful and looked at her.

"It's bajtra." The man purred as he slid into the seat opposite them. "You looked like you could use it." Jayne almost felt Gaby soften as she looked across the table and into the eyes that had caught her off guard in London. "Oh damn, I've left my cigarettes on the bar." He got up to leave but Gaby jumped to her feet.

"I'll go and get them." She trotted off towards the bar. Jayne lifted the glass and shot him an enquiring look.

"You spent an evening with Doug. I guessed you would have drunk this before. He had to get it imported into Hell; we didn't have anything close to that horse piss." Nick took a quick glance towards the bar. "We don't have long. I've set you up with the man at the end booth."

"You've what?"

"I think he's our killer. He usually operates out of Madrid but he's down here doing a one-off job for some person who is dictating when they die. His target won't leave the monastery. He must be our man." Nick garbled out his message as Gaby started to stride back towards the table, his cigarettes in her hand.

"If you could come back here and do all this then why am I here?"

"I can't help heaven for fuck's sake. How would that look?" He shot her a derisory glance.

"And yet here we are." Jayne replied.

Gaby placed the cigarettes and lighter onto the table and slid back into her seat.

"Thanks." Nick slid one out, put it between his lips and lit it. "Want one?"

"No thanks. I'll resist the temptation." Jayne replied, whilst Gaby reached out to take one. Nick needlessly cupped his hands around the end of the cigarette as he lit it, letting his fingers rest against Gaby's.

"Will you come and join us? My friend is at the other end of the bar. We could do with some company." Nick indicated the booth in the darkest recess at the other end of the room.

"Sure." Gaby oozed and Jayne tried to hide the fact she was rolling her eyes. It was quite alarming how seductive Nick was being without even really appearing to try. Were demonic people always so tempting? She slid along the seat and followed the two of them down the room.

"Santiago, I've found us some company. Can I introduce..." Nick managed to stop himself, realising that he shouldn't actually know her name.

"Julie." Jayne went to slide along the seat opposite the seated man. Gaby shot her daggers. She changed tack and slid in beside the stranger.

"And Gaby." Gaby shuffled along the seat ending up opposite the man, Nick sat down beside her, casually laying his arm along the back of the seat. Jayne swore she could almost see Gaby melt a little.

"And you are?" Jayne looked across at Nick.

"I am Enrique." Nick waved at the bar man and four glasses of a dark cherry coloured liquid appeared, ice clinking. Nick took up his glass and turned to talk to Gaby.

Santiago raised his eyebrows at the two opposite him, reached across for the drink, and tapped his glass against Jayne's.

"Eskerriska!"

"So, what do you do Santiago?"

"You mean when I'm not letting strange men set me up with women in bars." His eyes seemed to smile but his face remained motionless. "I'm a mechanic; I fix things." He took a mouthful of the liquid and then swirled the ice around the glass, as though he thought the remainder needed diluting. "And you?"

"I'm staying up at the monastery. They have got me working in the paramor." Jayne let a small amount of the liquid slip down her throat. It brought back memories of cough medicine.

"Hah, you can change my sheets tomorrow." Santiago left his gaze just a little too long on Jayne. She wasn't sure what to read into that comment, if anything. "Why are you working at the monastery? You don't seem like..." He flicked his hand across the table, towards Gaby. "The normal type."

"I wanted to get away. I needed somewhere cheap where I could just forget...him." Jayne had worked for some time that afternoon on her back story. She was going with jilted lover. There was a pause.

"Revenge rebound sex is more of his department." Santiago tilted his glass across the table towards the others. Nick and Gaby seemed oblivious to the fact that the other two had stopped talking and were watching them.

"I thought the two of you had just met." Jayne thought it best not to reply directly to the previous comment. Santiago gave a little laugh.

"No, we have known each other for years, we are in similar lines of work. I wasn't expecting to bump into him here but he does have a habit of turning up in odd places." He downed his drink. "Anyway, I am working and you are drunk. If you are back here tomorrow night after 8, I'll see if I can help you." He gave a grin. Similar lines of work? Jayne tried to see if there was even the faintest glimpse of orange or red around his eyes. Was this all a big demonic trap? She realised she had been staring straight into his eyes for a little too long.

"Oh, I'm sure you could." Santiago let out a loud laugh and a genuine smile crossed his face. He reached over to tap Nick on the arm.

"Mantentzeko inork bero hau niretzat." Nick let a grin spread across his face and then Jayne sensed it almost stopped as he wondered whether she understood that they were saying. She didn't. Santiago turned back to her. "Excuse me, I must leave." Jayne slid out of the seat to let him past. "Until tomorrow night." He slid a hand behind her neck and pulled her in to kiss her. Jayne didn't resist. She thought it would be a bit out of character given her last comment. It wasn't entirely unenjoyable.

*

212

"Do you think we could sneak Enrique back into the room?" Gaby reached around Jayne to get a hand towel.

"What the hell for?"

"Oh come on. It would be fun." Gaby pushed her gently and grinned into the rest room mirror over her shoulder. "He said you wouldn't be up for it."

"He was right." Jayne smoothed back the sections of her hair that had escaped from the pony tail. "Are you ready to head back? We need to met Mel."

"Ok. I think Enrique will walk us back."

"I bet he will." Jayne muttered under her breath. The fact that Santiago claimed he has known Nick for years had thrown her. There had to be some plan behind all of this but she couldn't see it.

"Oh come on. You must admit he's more fun than the do gooders at the monastery." Gaby pointed behind her.

"Oh, he's defiantly not a do gooder." Jayne smiled back at her new friend who seemed to take the comment as an endorsement of her date.

44

Jayne lifted the fresh towels out of the cupboard and stacked them into the trolley. There were only three rooms in the parador being used at the moment. Apparently, more were expected in next week but that didn't really concern her; she was planning to leave later tonight. By seven thirty her mission would either be a success or a failure, either way there was no need to stay. Martin had given her fairly specific instructions. As little interaction as possible, preferably none. She was fairly sure an evening in the bar probably counted as interaction. Although, to be fair, it hadn't actually been with the man they were back here to find; he didn't leave the monastery. She checked the rest of the supplies on the trolley and started down the corridor. It was nearly ten o'clock. The first guest had already left. The other two occupied rooms were at the end of the corridor.

"Room service." She knocked on the door, waited a second and then let herself in.

"Hola." Santiago sat in the chair by the window, his feet resting on the table. He didn't move as she came in.

"Shall I come back?" He looked up lazily, a smile slowly spreading across his face.

"No, carry on. Don't bother changing the sheets." He sat back and watched her as she went about smoothing out the sheets and making the bed. There was something very unnerving about being watched so closely. "Are you doing the room next door?"

Jayne made a show of checking her sheet but she knew fine well that she was scheduled to clean that room too. That was the room she suspected held their target person.

"Yes. It's the same as here, just a quick bed make and a clean of the bathroom.

"Get your stuff." Santiago lowered his legs and reached out to take her hand. "I'll take you in. He can be a bit strange." He led her out into the corridor and along to the door at the end. He knocked and then pulled a key from his pocket and let himself in.

"Miguel!" The room was in darkness, the shutters still closed. "Miguel, gela zerbitzua, servicio de habitaciones." There was a movement in the corner as the occupant reached over to open the shutters and turned to face them. He was maybe late thirties, dressed in black jeans with a black shirt, short dark hair framing an attractive face, the eyes of which were undeniably tinged with orange. He waved Jayne towards the bed and started to converse with Santiago in a language Jayne could not comprehend. She made a few mental notes. There was a space under the bed, there was a wardrobe in the room, suitable places to hide but how would she get into the room if he never left? She busied herself as the two men had a rather animated conversation.

45

"Ah Mr Metcalfe, do come in." Joshua waved the man into his office. Alarm bells started ringing in Simon's head. People only ever used his surname if something was wrong, very wrong indeed.

"Do take a seat. How is the Dali Lama case going?"

"On target." Simon sunk down into the leather chair, usually it felt comfortable and supportive, today it felt restrictive.

"Would it panic you at all if I told you that the Dali Lama in Washington has requested a private meeting with the American President for tomorrow night?"

"Yes, Sir It would." Simon flipped open his notepad and started scribbling. "When for?"

"7.30. Is there anything else you would like to tell me about the case?"

"Well, basically we have identified the soul of the Dali Lama. He is down in Ilford and not about to come to any harm. We think we have identified the soul that is in Washington."

"Think?" Joshua prompted.

"We are 99% sure that the soul is Miguel Eltordo. He was a Spanish partisan in the Napoleonic wars who escaped from Hell forty eight years ago. When he was thirty he died and somehow managed to be placed into the body of the present Dali Lama, displacing the Dali Lama's soul into a boy who happened to be born in the village whilst his parents were on holiday. This left a soul over which ties in with the records from that department. We are concentrating on changing that sequence of events."

"You are very..." Joshua thought about his next word carefully. "Is it diplomatic, the word that I am looking for?" He pushed himself to his feet. "Yes, you are very diplomatic. You have told me everything whilst telling me nothing. There is an art to that. I have been practicing it for years. You think Doug and I tell Michael everything that is going on, oh no, defiantly not. That is why I can spot it a mile off. Mind you, I was given a bit of a hint in this case."

"A hint?" Simon swivelled in his chair to follow Joshua as he walked around the room.

"I have just had Doug in here." Joshua stopped at the window and looked out at the view, his hands clasped behind his back.

"Doug?"

"Yes." Joshua moved over to the drinks cabinet, thought about it and decided against it. "He's resigned."

"Resigned!" Simon's notebook fell to the floor.

"Yes, resigned. Less than a day after I persuade him to come back and take over the entire training operation he walks in here and tells me he has killed his trainee and resigned. Now maybe we could run through the case again and you could fill in all the missing bits."

46

"What do you mean, resigned?" Martin was lying on the sofa, a bottle of beer beside him, a packet of cigarettes lying on his stomach, watching the television.

"Gone, packed up and left. His office is completely empty and only Joshua knows where he is." Simon was busy packing all the essential stuff they would need back in heaven. Joshua couldn't see any point in them staying down on Earth. There was nothing more they could do down here. The plan was to catch a flight to Edinburgh and use the portal that they had in a flat there. The transport system was still not 100%.

"That man is always running away." Martin lit another cigarette. They had a no smoking policy in heaven so he took his trips to Earth as an opportunity to feed his habit.

"Ah, now lets see why. Could it be because he is just back out of rehab, kind of makes up with the man who is the reason that he went to Hell in the first place, and also the man who put him in rehab, meets a nice girl only to find that the man he thought was a friend has actually killed his new girlfriend, as well shooting his wife, whist he wasn't looking."

"Yeah alright," snapped Martin "the way everybody goes on about it you would think I did it on purpose." He took a lungful of smoke and blew it up towards the ceiling. "If he hadn't been looking when I shot his wife, we might not be in quite such a mess."

"I just hope Jayne pulls it off for your sake or we can add the assassination of the President of the United States of America to your list of screw ups for this mission." Simon pulled the zip on his bag shut. "Will you get a move on. I've booked us in for dinner at Gino's with Hans. He thinks he might have picked her up on a monitor." Martin's ears pricked up.

"If he has got her on the monitor we must have some influence over her."

"He is not hopefully. The best he can offer us is the opportunity to watch her die."

"No." Martin jumped to his feet, over the sofa and up to Simon. "If we have got her on monitors we can do something." He reached over and grabbed the bag that Simon had just closed. "Are we going then? I've got people I need to see before Gino's." With that he walked out of the flat leaving Simon to lock up and chase after him.

47

Jayne sat on the bench finishing her soup as the others stacked their bowls and returned to their work. Her work in the parador had finished in the middle of the morning and so she had helped out in the kitchen preparing the soup for the workers.

Gaby picked up the pile of bowls and joined her on the short walk back to the kitchen.

"Julie, can you do me a favour? I've got to go and help clear the bottom field."

"Sure, what is it?"

"I told Enrique I would meet him down at the bridge into the forest at 2 but I'm not going to make it. Could you pop along and explain."

"Can't you just phone him?" Jayne dumped the soup bowl into the sink and set the taps running.

"I don't have his number. It won't take you long, just run along and tell him we will be down in the bar at 9." Gaby grabbed her arm. "Please, I don't want him thinking I'm not interested."

"Sure." Jayne would quite like to bump into Nick again and see if he had any idea as to how to stop or delay the killing of Miguel. She still had a slight nagging doubt about the fact that Nick seemed to know the killer, that seemed a little too convenient. Maybe she could ask him about that as well.

"Thanks, you're an angel." Gaby gave her arm a squeeze and left the kitchen.

48

Vardeth glanced at the office clock again and returned to his pile of paper clips. He had been given one of those magnetic pyramids complete with its own selection of multi coloured paper clips. He was currently trying to see how tall a tower he could build. He had already seen how far he could build horizontally and investigated whether colour was related to strength of binding. Not that Vardeth was bored, good grief no, he just enjoyed playing with paperclips. He wasn't short of work; his desk was covered in open files, spare bits of paper covered in scribbled notes and an unending supply of doodles. Only this week he had been given personal responsibility for one of the most high powered jobs going. Oh yes, life was no bed of roses when you were in charge of a crack team of spectral warriors. No more taking control of the monster under the bed section for him, now he chased down wanted souls. He was a debt collector to people who had made deals with the devil and once a month he got to host the divisional coffee morning. He picked up the latest order and read it again. Capture angel currently on Earth who has emotional involvement with J. La Valette. It sounded simple enough. They had started with the obvious; watch Mr La Valette and see where he went. They had been watching him for two days now and he wasn't going anywhere, including visiting Earth. Vardeth wondered what sort of emotional involvement this was if it didn't involve seeing one another. The easiest and fastest plan had failed so they had started pulling out all the files they had on angels. Who had trained them and when and still they had come up with a big fat zero. He reached the top of the paper clip tower, there were no more paperclips. He glanced up at the notice board at the end of the office. Young Kevin had stuck pictures all over it. Kevin had seen too many police movies in Vardeth's opinion. He had read too many books. Kevin was trying to psychoanalyse Jacques La Vallete to work out what sort of person they were looking for. If Vardeth had leant one thing during all his time in Hell it was that people are complex and very unpredictable, which made psychoanalysis a bit of a waste of time. Of course, if Vardeth had wanted psychoanalysis he could have just pulled it out of the file on the attempted abduction and destruction of Mr la Valette, it was all there but Young Kevin seems to be having fun, why spoil it for him. There was a clatter outside the office. Vardeth pulled over a file with one hand and squashed his paperclip tower with the other. The door flew open.

"Kevin, I've told you about knocking before, can't you see that I am busy."

"Sorry Sir." Kevin attempted to shuffle to attention but in his excitement, he just moved across the floor a little.

"What is it Kevin?" Asked Vardeth in a tone that had already filed the answer as being on a par with the coffee machine being broken again.

"We have found her Sir."

"Who?" Vardeth had completely forgotten the file he had read only minutes before.

"La Valette angel Sir, we have found her." Vardeth was up, around the desk and beside Kevin before he had finished talking.

"Well don't hang around boy, take me to the monitors."

49

The bridge into the forest seemed a very strange place to arrange to meet someone. Even in the daylight of the early afternoon it had an ominous darkness about it. Nick was leaning on the balustrade looking into the water. He glanced up as Jayne approached, he raised his eyebrows in greeting

"This seems a strange place to arrange to meet someone. It's hardly conducive to a romantic get together." Jayne joined him leaning over the railing.

"I work for the Marquis de Sade Jayne; consent isn't high on my list of priorities."

"Oh." Jayne pushed herself away. One night in a bar and she had forgotten what Nick actually was and who he was working for. "Gaby can't come. She said she would see you in the bar tonight."

"We should be gone by then." He turned around, crossed his ankles and leant back against the bridge, squinting his eyes against the sunlight that was creepy in between the tree branches. "Any ideas how you are going to do it?"

"None." She paused. "Can't you just intervene?"

"I can't help you Jayne." Nick took on the tone one might adopt for a child who keeps asking the same question

"You want this Miguel back don't you?"

"I do, but he is planning something devious. I can't stop that. That is your department." Silence fell on the pair.

"You know Santiago. He says you're in similar lines of work." Jayne's words broke the silence. Jayne had taken Santiago's description of himself as a 'mechanic' in the Hollywood meaning of the word.

"I'm fucking demonic Jayne. It surprises you that I kill people?"

"No, wait, you actually kill people?" Jayne looked at Nick in disbelief.

"It's what I did to end up like this. It's what I drive people to do to each other now." Nick pushed himself up off of the bridge. "Shall we head back? It appears I'm not going to get what I came here for." He extended his hand towards the path.

"No wait!" Jayne stood in his way. "This all seems a little too convenient. The only way we can stop this Lama thing is for me to come back here and then when I get here it turns out the killer we are trying to stop is an old mate of yours and actually you could have come back here and stopped it yourself. I know you don't want to, but you could have."

"Jayne." Nick took a step towards her, "I have been alive for hundreds of years, I move in the sort of circles where I met people like Santiago. I used to be Santiago. I agree there are a whole load of things that seem to have gone wrong with this mission that need some explaining but for now we just need to concentrate on getting this done and then getting you out of here before they arrive."

"They?" There was a moments silence as Nick realised that Martin hadn't brought Jayne entirely up to speed. Was there anyone who knew the full story?

"The spectral warriors have been activated to find you." He moved her out of his path and strode up the path towards the field.

"Is that bad?"

"Oh fuck yeah. It doesn't get much worse." She ran around in front of him and blocked his path. She put out her two hands and he walked forward until his chest was against them.

"Why do they want me?" She stared up into his face and he almost felt a twinge of compassion.

"They want Doug."

"How do they know about Doug and I?" Nick could feel the accusation in the sentence.

"They don't. They just know he is training you. If they find out you are any more then they will double their efforts to get you." He pushed her hands down and continued up the path.

"Is there a plan?"

"Come up with an idea to delay that killing, even by a second, and then I get you the hell out of here before they arrive."

"I thought you didn't want to help me?"

Nick turned and smiled. "And yet here we are."

50

"There, do you see?" Kevin pointed to the faint green blob on the monitor screen. "That's her."

"What makes you think that?" Vardeth peered at the monitor.

"The readings aren't quite right. She isn't reading as a mortal but she isn't tagged. I checked with our contacts and La Valette was apparently seen entering her apartment block last week." Kevin glossed over the fact that he was also seen leaving the building. Why let the facts spoil a good story.

"But Kevin, this is showing almost twenty years ago." Vardeth punched a button and the date appeared at the top of the screen.

"They sent her back in time." Kevin's grin spread so far across his face it looked as though his face was going to split in two.

"Back in time." Vardeth drummed his fingers on the console. Why were they going to such trouble to hide this person?

"Yes Sir. I was down here the other day watching this monitor when suddenly that blob just appeared. There were two to start with but then one of them disappeared, leaving her behind. The other blob wasn't there for long enough for us to trace it for any details. Someone took her back to here." It crossed Vardeth's mind to ask why Kevin was watching a monitor of eighteen years ago in Spain but he let it go, somethings were better not knowing.

"Alright Kevin, get the boys together. We are going in."

51

"Very nice." Gaby came into the bedroom still holding a piece of bread. "I thought I didn't see you at dinner." She walked around Jayne as she smoothed down her clothes and had another look in the mirror.

"I'm going to go and see Santiago."

"You can't wait until the bar tonight?" Gaby threw herself down on her bed. "Actually, I don't think we will be seeing you at the bar tonight, will we?"

"Does it look too much?" Jayne turned around. She was wearing a simple cotton dress that she had found in the back of the housekeepers cupboard. She wasn't sure if it was lost property or whether it had belonged to the previous housekeeper. She had left the top few buttons undone so that her cleavage was clearly on show and she had also undone a few buttons at the bottom so that her thighs were visible as she walked.

"It depends what you're after." Gaby stood up and walked around her, slowly inspecting the get up. "If you are going to meet his parents then it's defiantly too much. I think it's probably ideal for what you have in mind." She reappeared at the front and gave Jayne a big grin. "Go and knock him dead."

52

"Gentlemen, gentlemen, do come in." Joshua rose from his chair as Simon and Martin entered the room. "I thought we could all watch proceedings in here." He waved his hand around the meetings room. The room was set back off of the balcony of Hans' monitoring room. The wall to the balcony was covered in blinds, the opposite wall covered in monitors that relayed the screens down in the main monitoring room. The table in the centre was laid for dinner. "It's still early, so I have had a meal arranged." He brought his gaze down to the two of them. "I've cancelled your table at Gino's." He indicated for them to take their places. A silent Hans already sat at the far end. "The right screen shows Washington, in fact the President's Office. The left screen shows some God forsaken place in Spain. Might I suggest that if you try this again Martin, and you won't by the way, you introduce some element of time warp. Send them back in the evening to the morning of the day in question then at least you have twelve hour's notice of what is going to happen."

"Pardon?" Martin raised a quizzical eyebrow.

"Explain Hans." Joshua waved to the seated German.

"Well." Hans peered over his glasses. "Jayne was sent back exactly eighteen years. She is in exactly the same time frame as us just eighteen years ago. The Dali Lama in Washington has requested a meeting with the President at 7.30 because that is the precise time at which he was born. Whoever is behind this has put a lot of thought in to protecting their plan.

We have a scenario here that at 7.29 the bad Dali Lama will knock on that door and we won't know who is going to walk into the room until they do walk into the room. If you had sent Jayne back eighteen years and a half day, still to the time she arrived then she would have been out of time shift, her morning would be our evening so we would have known who was going to walk through that door several hours before they did." Hans anticipated the question that was forming on Simon's lips. "The normal time difference between countries is automatically taken into consideration when you time travel with our system."

"Still, all adds to the excitement!" Joshua glanced down the table at Martin. "We can add it to the list of screw ups."

53

The soul of Miguel Eltordo sat on the edge of the seat in the body of the Dali Lama. He needed to get this over with quickly. There was obviously some residual goodness left inside this body. The longer he sat and waited the more and more he began to doubt the wisdom of his plan. He had been trapped in here for eighteen years. He was the youngest ever Dali Lama to take such an active role in world peace. Little did they know that he was now within striking distance of his final aim. He patted the gun and the bowl as they sat under the layers of orange cloth. At least that part of his plan was correct; no one would search the Dali Lama. Soon he would be alone with the President of the free world. A quick tranquilliser and a soul swap and he would have untold power. He would be able to reactivate his old network that he had left in the hands of his old loyal friend Heraldo and together they could wreak havoc.

"Mr Dali Lama, Sir." Said the guard in the way that only an American can. "The President will see you now." Miguel rose to his feet and stated the long walk towards the office at the other side of the building.

54

It was 7.25 when Jayne got up the courage to knock in the door and prayed that Santiago was still inside. The door opened. He stood framed in the light of the table lamp and slowly looked her up and down before stopping at her face with a large grin and raised eyebrows.

"Hola."

"Hola." She put her hand onto his chest and pushed him back into the room, knocking the door shut behind them with her foot.

"I was just on my way out." He looked down to his chest as her hand slid between his shirt buttons and flicked them undone. There was almost a shudder of a laugh.

"Can't it wait a moment." Jayne peered up at him through her fringe trying her best to look seductive and then followed it up by reaching up to kiss him. He submitted, reaching an arm around her to pull her lower back into him. It was at this point Jayne realised she hadn't really thought this through. He pulled back.

"I would love to do this but I have to go and do something."

Jayne paused. Was he seriously considering going next door and killing someone and then coming back to continue this?

"You can do something here." He laughed and kissed her again.

"Trust me, I would much rather do this something, but it doesn't pay the bills." He squeezed her into him, spun her around a little and then withdrew his hand, allowing Jayne to fall back onto the bed. She saw the small glance towards the clock. Was he swithering? She pushed herself up to a reclined sitting position and wound her legs around his. He looked down at her and glanced at the clock again. Santiago reached out and gently touched the bits of her hair that had fallen down at the side of her face. He let his hand slide down her neck and trace the edge of the neckline until it came to the buttons at the front. He flicked the button undone and then stroked his hand back towards her neck, tracing the top of her bra cup. Jayne caught her breath.

The door bounced off of the wall and Miguel stood there. He took one look at the situation and launched a tirade of what sounded like Spanish. Santiago looked down at Jayne, he glanced at Miguel, shrugged and then reached behind him and produced a gun that must have been in his waist band. He reached out and pointed it at Miguel whilst his legs were still entwined by Jayne's. They all looked at the clock.

55

Jocheim saw the men running up the path. They had a strange quality. He couldn't tell how many men there were, sometimes it looked like a dozen at other times they seemed to morph into only three or four. He rubbed his eyes and looked again, half expecting them to have disappeared. They were led by an enthusiastic young man and an elder, equally hopefully looking, man dressed in a similar black coat to himself.

They slowed as they approached him.

"Do you have a recently arrived young woman here?" Jocheim's heart fell. He had high hopes for his new arrival. Surely she wasn't another of these people using the monastery as a hiding place from the authorities. He had had quite a few of them over the past three years. He had dithered the first time as to whether the monastery ought to act as a sanctuary for these misguided youths. He had changed his mind when he found the drug factory in the basement,

"What has she done?"

"She's here then?" The elder man stopped in front of him. Jocheim felt as though his soul had been gripped by some dark force and he subconsciously reached for the crucifix around his neck.

"Please tell us where she is." Kevin gasped. They had had to materialise outside of the monastery and he hadn't performed this much physical activity since he had died.

"Tell is where she is or your soul will rot in eternal torment." One of the unspecified number of people behind them materialised as a face and looked Jocheim in the eye before melting back into the crowd behind them.

"What he said." Kevin breathlessly waved a hand towards the spirit. Jocheim looked from Kevin to the other man and something deep inside him told him that they were capable of condemning his soul for all eternity.

"She's in the parador, through the courtyard and then around to the left."

56

"No!" Jayne pulled her legs up and jumped up to stand between the gun and Miguel. Santiago raised one eyebrow.

"Santiago! Mátame ahora! Lo debe ser ahora! Dispárame a través de ella!" Jayne didn't need Spanish to know that that didn't sound good. Santiago flicked the barrel of the gun.

"Get out of the way. I have to shoot him."

"Dispárame!"

"Move!" Jayne took a few steps back so that she was out of the reach of Santiago's arm as he tried to swipe her sideways onto the bed.

"Dispárame!"

"Don't make me..." Santiago let a pleading look cross his face, briefly.

"Dispárame a través de ella!" Santiago shrugged and pulled the trigger. He was aiming for a warning shot, something that would make her move out of the way and then he could get a clean shot at Miguel. The revolver bit back into his hand, there was a scream and then a thud as the bullet burrowed into the wall.

Jayne felt a tug at her dress. She kept her eyes on Santiago. His eyes looked at her but the whites became more visible. Something had happened. She glanced down to the cotton fabric at her side. The flesh was exposed with a neat groove of skin missing. It should have been pumping blood all over the floor but there was nothing, not a drop.

"Santiago." Miguel dived out from behind her. He would have been in time if Santiago had been drawn and ready but the gun was at his side, his eyes on Jayne's stain free dress.

"Who are you? Do you realise what you have done?" Miguel turned on Jayne, the red in his eyes even more visible now. The wound at her side told him exactly who she was, or at least where she had come from. "I'm not going back. I will fill you so full of lead that won't be able to patch you up." He cast his gaze around for a weapon and then made a grab for Santiago, who was standing dumbstruck by the lack of blood and his victims sudden ability to speak fluent English. Jayne dived down the side of the bed. She slid up towards the top of the bed and banged into a bottle of champagne nestling in an ice bucket. This must be the planned celebration for after the job had been done. She wondered for a moment whether Santiago had planned to share it with her. She hefted out the bottle and, remembering Martin's advice, she got to her feet muttering and emptied the contents over the struggling men.

57

Santiago heard a blood curdling scream and felt a large gust of wind. He was sure he caught a glimpse of Enrique at the window, which was impressive as they were on the first floor, and then his bedroom door flew open again and several men dressed in black ran in. He stood at the end of the bed dripping, not sure what was going on and thankful that he had been paid upfront for this job.

"So, Kevin. What went wrong?" The elder man in a black cassock asked as he stalked into the room, his eyes searching for something.

"She is not here." Kevin peered into the scope of one of his latest toys.

"You mean she ceased to exist?"

"Could be." He scanned the room again, walking around the dripping figure of Santiago. "Certainly no reading here."

"You do have a gift for the obvious." Vardeth shifted uneasily in front of his band of spectral warriors. "I hope you have something a little more convincing when you have to explain this to Beelzebub." He walked over and had a quick glance under the bed, ever hopeful. "Oh well, no point hanging around here." He walked over to the door with a backwards glance at the dripping figure at the end of the bed. "Come on boys." Vardeth led the spectral warriors out of the room leaving Kevin wondering why he had suddenly been prompted to the one who reported to Beelzebub.

"What happened?" Santiago asked just as Kevin was about to leave.

"I'm not sure. We think we lost an angel." With that Kevin left.

Santiago fell onto the bed. He had no idea what had just happened. His hand fell down the side of the bed and touched the bottle of champagne. Oh well, the job was over, the client had gone and the money was in the bank. Time to celebrate.

58

"What happened?" Martin jumped from his seat and ran up to the monitor. It showed one green blob and twelve purple.

"She has gone." Joshua wiped his mouth with a napkin.

"Gone?" Martin turned to face him.

"I had Hans lock onto her. At 7.32 she was going to be transported onto that monitor." Joshua pointed to the black screen. "As you can see, she is not there and she is not in Spain so I think it would be fair to conclude that she has gone."

"And these guys?" Martin indicated over his shoulder.

"The green blob I suspect is the assassin and the twelve purple blobs would be the squad of spectral warriors." Hans patted his mouth with a napkin and shrugged.

"Spectral warriors?" Martin couldn't remember the last time he had heard of spectral warriors turning up in force like that. He knew they were after her but they were usually like tax inspectors; you never actually saw them in person.

"They must have found her."

"So, if she has been captured by spectral warriors, we could still go and save her." Martin let a small hopeful smile cross his face.

"If she had been captured Martin, she would still be on the screen. She has gone." Hans rose from the table. "I expect we lost here somewhere between Spain and that screen. The system wasn't built for time travelling untagged angels." Hans changed his glare to a glance at Joshua. "May I be excused now Sir?"

"Certainly." Joshua watched as the man left. Hans was in charge of transportation and he didn't like to see it go wrong. Joshua felt a slight pang of guilt for his little theatrical performance. "Your saving grace could be the fact that the target seems to have disappeared as well and yet there are still two people on the monitor showing Washington." He pointed to the right hand screen. "Keep watching that and report to my office tomorrow morning at nine."

"Sir?"

"I've got a contact number for Doug. I think someone should tell him what's happened, don't you?" With that Joshua left, leaving a piece of paper containing a number on the table.

59

"The President hopes that you are well." The aide whispered in to the Dali Lama's ear. He sat still, silent and confused. He was in Washington, at the conference of religious leaders, but he was sure he hadn't been here a minute ago.

"You wanted to see me?" The President rose from behind his desk and came around to greet his visitor. He had seemed such a composed fellow the other day. He hadn't even flinched at that attempt on his life but now he seemed a little bewildered.

"I did?" The Lama smiled sweetly and tried to remember why he had requested to see the President. "I did." He confirmed. "May I present you with this Tibetian prayer bowl." He pulled the bowl from under his wraps. "We can put all the good of the world into it to preserve it for ever." He bowed low and presented the bowl to the President who took it with a dutiful smile. The Lama was more composed than he could ever imagine.

Willis pulled his arm up to his face and spoken into his cuff.

"Make a note to search all the religious leaders. This guy has just pulled a bowl from his shirt sleeve. He could have had anything up there."

60

Doug sat on the stone edge of the balcony and looked out over the rolling fields to the coast line and the horizon beyond. He heard the front door to the heaven side of the house open. It would be Martin, he was sure of that. Anyone else would have just telephoned but Martin had a thing about talking face to face, especially if it was bad news. Doug smirked to himself. It was somewhat ironic considering that Martin had said very little to his face for the past year.

"Come through Martin, I'm out here." The door to the living room slid open and Martin appeared with his hands thrust deep into his baseball jacket pockets.

"X ray vision, is that a recent development mate." He grinned although he was feeling anything other than happy.

"I knew it would be you. Well?" Doug continued to stare at the horizon, cradling an empty beer bottle in his hands, despite the early hour.

"Yes thanks, and yourself?" Martin shrugged off his jacket, threw it over one of the patio chairs and disappeared back into the house, heading for the kitchen. He was used to Doug's flat; he had spent many days here in the past.

Doug let the obvious twisting of his comments go. He raised his voice so that Martin could still hear him.

"I had Courtney here last night."

"Courtney?" Martin asked from the kitchen.

"Courtney from STC."

"Oh that Courtney." Martin said, still none the wiser.

"Courtney from the space time continuum unit." Doug pushed himself off of the ledge and followed the aroma of fresh coffee into the kitchen. "Do you know the probability of your stunt actually working?"

"Next to nothing I expect." Martin pushed a steaming espresso mug across the counter to Doug.

"It isn't next to nothing Martin, it is completely nothing. It will never work properly. If Jayne manages to stop this bloke dying at the right time then Courtney reckons that there would be such a violent reaction that rather than flipping the Earth onto a parallel existence it would just change the Dali Lama. You would have some poor bloke down there who as far as he is concerned will just have been dumped into his present existence." Martin stood in silence as Doug rattled on.

"Did you understand it when he explained it?" Doug stared back in reply. It was one of Martin's infamous disarming comments. Doug let out a sigh and ran his hands back through his hair.

"No, not really." Doug swapped the beer bottle for the coffee. "He was going on about worm holes and existence blankets." Doug ran his hand over his face. "It sounded pretty bad."

"Well, it does seem to have worked." Martin did not smile, "he will be able to cope with just being dumped into his life eighteen years on, he's religious for heavens sake." He took a mouthful of coffee. He had missed Doug's coffee maker over the past few years.

"And Jayne?" There wasn't any hope in Doug's question it was just a reminder to Martin that not everything had worked.

"Ah." Martin picked up his mug and rushed after Doug as he returned to the balcony. "I am sorry mate, I had no idea."

"How did you know I was here?" Doug changed the subject.

"I recognised the phone number that Joshua gave me. He thought I should tell you about..." Martin gazed down into the garden, "is that the olive we planted?"

Doug glanced up at his face and then followed his finger towards a lone tree in the corner of the garden.

"Yes." They had planted it the first time Martin had come to the house. He and four other angel recruits had come for the weekend to learn the importance of their work, the rules of conduct.

"I am so sorry about Jayne mate. She was a really nice girl." Martin had been working on what to say on the way to the house. He had realised he had to say something. If he had learnt one thing from the events of the last year it was that.

Doug let out a little sigh.

"Tell me one thing Martin. How did you overload the system?"

"You don't think..."

"How did you do it?" Doug's gaze remained on his, now empty, coffee cup.

"I cut my finger and put it in her mouth." Martin correctly decided that this was not a moment for humour, for once in his life.

"She knew she might not come back." Doug stared out towards the sea again. "That is why she asked me to stay that night. She must have wanted to go or she could have told me how to get her home. She knew that we had a transport that was working. She was so bloody confident. She was a lot like you." He turned to look at Martin. "That's why I thought she would make a good agent. She was so confident that she could do anything. You know most people when they arrive in heaven take a few weeks to acclimatise, that's why they make the training so damn long, not her, she seemed to take it all in her stride.

"She did seem to bounce back from anything you threw at her." Martin recalled the meetings with Nick, the explanation of the plan, even when she found herself trapped down there in the first place.

"Well one thing is for sure." Doug glanced in his coffee cup, hopeful that there was something left. "She sure as hell ain't going to bounce back from this."

61

"Will you lie still." The plea was whispered into Jayne's ear as she came to. She complied and tried to compose her thoughts. She remembered struggling to her feet with the ice bucket and throwing the contents over the two struggling men. She remembered a scream, a large gust of wind that blew her off her feet, smacking her head on the edge of the bedside table and then, just as her vision started to close in, a large number of men running into the room.

"Where am I? Who are you?" A warm hand pressed down over her mouth, silencing her and a pair of smouldering orange eyes appeared above her.

"It's me, Nick, and we are in a cupboard in my flat." He held a finger to his lips to indicate he would like silence. He removed the other hand from her mouth and returned to gazing through a crack in the doors.

Jayne sat staring into the gloom. As her eyes became accustomed to it she could pick out trouser legs and shirt sleeves. Well, this was certainly a turn up for the books; she was still alive, or at least still dead, and in a wardrobe. It was certainly more than she had hoped for.

"They've gone." Nick pushed open the door and tumbled out onto the floor. "Now, What the fuck were you playing at?" He turned on Jayne and she saw the same flare at the edge of his eyes that she had seen in Miguel's. "Which part of not interacting with them includes trying to seduce the killer? I'm not convinced that you are working for the right side, you seem to have the morals of a Tom cat."

"What could I do? You set me up with him..." Jayne started in her defence.

"Not to do that, I didn't." Nick retaliated.

"I had to come up with something....hang on, you appeared at just the right moment. Where you watching me? Oh my god, you were going to watch!"

"Don't turn this into a thing about me. It's defiantly a thing about you." Nick disappeared out of the room and came back with what looked like a medical kit. "Get your dress off and let's sort that wound."

"What was I meant to do?" Jayne reached up to undo the dress buttons, thought twice about it in the presence of Nick and continued anyway.

"You could have just walked into the room. You didn't need to go in there and lay it all out for him." Nick produced a bottle from the bag and threw it across to her. Instant skin was written across the bottle in red. Jayne tipped it sideways to read the instructions. 'Had a nasty graze, cut yourself shaving again. Just paint a little instant skin along the affected area and watch that dead skin come to life. In 24 hours, a new patch of skin will have covered the site. Application can be repeated every 24 hours. If symptoms persist consult your doctor. She unscrewed the top and, with the attached brush, painted a little either side of the groove. The bullet must have almost missed, there was just a little groove across the side of her waist where it had caught her on the way past.

"Don't tell me you have never done what it takes to get an end result."

"I'm a fucking demon! It's expected!" Nick took the bottle back and popped it back in the bag.

"Your language has gone downhill." Jayne scolded as she pulled her dress back on and looked around the flat. It looked more like a show home, lots of shiny black surfaces and a bold red carpet. There was no mess anywhere. She gave a little inward laugh; this level of housekeeping would indeed be Hell.

"I usually moderate it around Martin."

"And you don't feel the need to moderate it around me?" She gave him a challenging stare.

"In view of your recent conduct, no."

"Well, no one has to know about it. We can just keep it between us." Jayne hadn't anticipated actually making it out of the situation in Spain and hadn't given any thought to any consequences of her actions. Nick stopped what he was doing and stared at her.

"Do not make deals with demons. That will result in nothing but trouble. If we get you back then you need to disclose everything and then I might not mention how much fun it looked like you were having." He gave a wicked grin.

"Well." Jayne pondered over what sounded an awful lot like blackmail. "He was no Doug..."

"Spare me the details." Nick returned the bag to the other room and walked up to the window. "We need to work out a way to get you across to that building." He pointed across to a large building the other side of a grassy square. Jayne joined him at the window. The view looked very familiar, buildings around a central square. It looked almost like the centre of heaven, the square opposite the headquarters.

"Where are we?" Jayne felt she already knew the answer but she needed it to be confirmed.

"That's Hell." Nick smirked as he felt the girl beside him stiffen.

"Hell?"

"Yep, I was limited as to where I could get you out to. Our system is not as sensitive as yours. I can transport people whether they are tagged or not."

"Then why didn't you transport me to Spain?"

"Again, I'm a fucking demon Jayne. I'm not going to help you."

"And yet here we are." Jayne looked back out of the window and shuddered at the fact that she wouldn't have been able to tell the difference between heaven and hell unless it had been pointed out. She had kind of hoped the difference would be obvious.

"Circumstances have changed." Nick pulled back the edge of the curtain and looked around the area. "They have searched this flat three times in the last week. I don't think they are on to anything but I don't want to hang around here more than we have to."

"What's changed?" Jayne's question brought him back to the previous comment.

"What? Oh, Doug has resigned." There was a moments silence.

"Over me?"

"I assume so." Nick gave her a smile "He could change his mind when he hears about Santiago."

"Why do you care? Why are you helping me now?"

"Having Doug in charge of angel training will give me better people to work with, and against. It's selfish reasons." He looked out of the window again. "Shit!"

"What's wrong." Jayne joined him peering out of the window but he pushed her back into the room.

"Spectral warriors. Maybe they just happen to be passing or maybe they traced you somehow."

"Why do they want me?" Jayne sunk further back into the depths of the room. Were those the men she had seen running into the room in Spain.

"They have been after you since you first appeared on Earth. They found you in Spain somehow. I got you out just as they came into the room. I don't think they can track you but maybe they can track me. I thought I had removed everything. Martin knew they were on the case." Nick left the window and started rummaging around under the bed.

"The bastard, he didn't say anything."

"Well, what were you going to do about it?" Nick returned to the window, dragging her beside him, feeling a strange need to defend Martin. "See that building over there in the corner?"

"The big one with flags?"

"Yep, That is the embassy where Doug worked. We need to get you inside that building." The building sat back from the square at the top of a short staircase. It looked like most embassies that Jayne had seen on Earth; a little plaque on the outside, flags and a non-descript facade.

"Can we just transport in?"

"Strangely enough, I cannot transport into heaven's territory. The closest I can get you is about 100 metres away. How fast can you cover that distance?"

"I've no idea." Jayne looked at the square. 100 metres, was that about half of the distance of one of the sides?

"Can you cover it quicker with those guys chasing you." Nick pointed towards the spectral warriors who did appear to be organising themselves and pointing at various buildings. "We need to go before they cordon off the embassy. Can you handle a weapon?"

"What did you have in mind?"

Nick pulled the lid off of the box that he had brought out from under the bed. Lying inside was an ancient sword. It was about the length of one of Jayne's legs with a beautifully carved hilt. She ran her fingers along the centre of the blade. Wrapping one hand around the hilt she lifted it from the box. It was deceptively light. She waved it in front of her and a light yellow flame seemed to lick up the sides of the blade.

"You are bloody kidding me!" Nick looked at her dumbstruck. "Do that again." She did it again and the flames played along the edge of the sword again. "That explains a lot." Nick pulled open the door of the wardrobe and rummaged at the back, eventually producing a pair of black gloves. "Put these on." He threw them across to her "and if you get back, tell Doug about that too." He shook his head and returned to the window. "Right, I'll get us as close as I can. When we arrive you need to locate that building and run as fast as you can. Do not look back. Don't worry about me just make sure you get into that building, and take this." He produced a little metal canister from his pocket.

"What is that?" Jayne took the offered package.

"It's the soul of Miguel Eltordo. Do not open it. When you get back hand it over to Doug and he can deal with it."

"How did you get it in here." Jayne shook the canister, expecting a rattle or a small voice to shout out.

"I'm guessing Martin gave you some liquid which you put on Santiago's gun." Nick had not been privy to the details of the plan.

"No, he just suggested I try blessing some water."

"He what?" Nick pulled back from the window and stared at her, a look of incredulity spreading across his face. Some of the suggestions that his colleague came out with were unbelievable.

"He suggested I bless some water." Jayne repeated.

"That shouldn't have worked." Nick ran his hand back through his hair and then shook his head. "I guess you ended up with Holy water. It doesn't usually have much effect on a mortal but if a damned soul is exposed to it, especially in the presence of an angel, it can be devastating." Nick looked out of the window again. They needed to get a move on. It looked like the spectral warriors had appeared in the square just by chance but it surely wouldn't take them long to realise a cordon around the embassy would be a smart move. Surely someone would have traced the link to Miguel by now. There was a chance to wrap up one of Hell's biggest mistakes and it seemed to be about to slip through their fingers. Nick was beginning to wonder what Jayne actually was because she clearly wasn't just an untrained angel rookie.

"Why don't you come with me?" The offer hit Nick as he stared down at the crowds in the square. There was silence. Was he considering her offer? Could he?

"It wouldn't work Jayne. I can't go to heaven. I'm a demon, I belong here. I'll run, they may eventually find me but I can withstand months of torture. You can't. We have to get you out of here." He smiled "but thanks for the offer." He returned to the window. "We need to go, they look like they are getting organised."

62

Jayne identified the building as the first blood curdling scream hit the air and she ran. Bullets flew past her. If she hadn't been shot in Spain she would have been panicking more but as it was she ran as fast as she could along the pavement towards the building at the corner, sword in one hand, metal container in the other.

"Gotcha." A hand gripped her shoulder. There was a scream and the hand flew down to her side, unattached.

"Run!" Nick screamed at her as she swung around to face the approaching crowd. She glimpsed him battling several figures and then turned and ran. She galloped up the steps taking two at a time and lunged for the large doorway. A hand took out her ankles and she fell onto the vestibule floor with a thud. It closed around one foot and started to pull her back out of the building. Jayne scrabbled for something to hold onto to stop her sliding across the tiles.

"Nick!" Her lungs ached from the running and the fall. "Nick!" But Nick had problems of his own. She could just make out a pile of people fighting at the bottom of the stairs. Nick was presumably at the bottom of that pile. She looked down at the warrior who was pulling at her ankles. Luckily the warriors were not quite what she had imagined they would be. They looked more like nerds in fancy dress. This one was still outside the large front doors, grinning inanely.

"Let me go!" Jayne tried to kick him off.

"You are joking, and lose my performance related pay, no way." Jayne had expected demonic babbling or something. This was just another person, like herself. With a massive effort she started to try and claw her way back along the tiled floor. It was hopeless. If she didn't end this soon the warrior would get assistance and she would be done for.

"Oh alright." Jayne released her hands and they both shot a few feet towards the stairs. Jayne remained on the top stair whilst the warrior dropped down a few stairs and lost his balance. His grip tightened around her leg as he fell. Jayne pulled the sword out from behind her and with one big swing that almost removed her own leg, she cut through the arm, turned and bolted for the door, the hand still firmly clasped around her ankle. She shot through the door in a dive, sliding across the floor and coming to rest with a thump against the reception desk.

"Yes." The man looked slowly over the edge of the desk towards the floor, as though he hadn't been aware of any previous disturbance.

"I am Jayne Pottage. I need to see the ambassador."

"Do you have an appointment?"

63

"What do you think he wants now?" Martin slumped against the side of the lift and stared up at the pattern of lights in the ceiling.

"I dread to think." Simon fiddled nervously with his jacket pockets.

"Maybe we are going to get the sack." Martin grinned as the lift doors slid effortlessly open. He waved at the secretary and headed straight for Joshua's office door.

"They don't sack angels do they?" Simon followed him. Martin opened the door and walked straight in without knocking.

"Here they are!" They both recognised Gabriel as soon as they entered. Joshua simply nodded at them. "I want to congratulate you both on a excellent job." Gabriel stalked over towards them and shook their hands. "Where is the other angel?"

"She is unable to join us at the moment." Michael spoke from a leather chair in which he was reclining. He was beaming from ear to ear, pleased that once again his angel squad had managed to deliver a solution for Gabriel.

"Well, I just wanted to thank you personally. I'll read the file after your debrief, but well done." Gabriel beamed at them and left the office a much happier man than he had been lately.

Michael raised himself from the chair and walked over to them.

"I'll hear about it all later but well done. I told Gabriel that you were the men for the job." He reached out and shook each of their hands. He gave Joshua a nod and followed Gabriel out of the room.

"They can both revise their opinions once they read the file." Joshua rose from his chair and stalked around the desk. "Sit down." They both obeyed. They were beginning to understand that dealings with Joshua were meant to be silent affairs on their behalf. "Luckily for you Martin someone saved your arse again. It must be embarrassing to be pulled from the claws of defeat so many times by Mr Metcalfe here, but to have it done by a rookie, a completely untrained angel who has only been dead a few days, and a woman to boot, that must be humiliating."

"I don't see it as much of a victory." It was so quiet that maybe it was intended as an internal thought.

"Pardon me?"

"I don't see it as much of a victory Sir." Martin wanted to sit back in the chair and relax but it just didn't seem appropriate and for once he was guided by that feeling.

"Really? Saving the world from complete destruction, preventing the assassination of one of the world leaders, that's not a victory? Setting our standards a little high aren't we Martin?" Joshua almost sneered the last sentence.

"With all due respect Sir, I risked, and lost, the existence of the trainee angel through my own misconduct."

"So what do you plan to do about it?" Joshua perched on the edge of his desk.

"I thought I might stop being an angel." Simon stared at Martin, this was the first he had heard of it. Joshua let out a little laugh.

"A noble gesture Martin, but totally needless. Your rookie reported in a few hours ago."

"How?" Martin and Simon exchanged glances.

"Well, I was rather hoping you could throw some light on that. You see, she turned up in Hell."

"She escaped from the spectral warriors?" Simon speculated although it seemed highly unlikely.

"Nice try but that doesn't really tie in with the eye witness accounts of a running street battle with swords and guns. Not only did she report in to the embassy but she brought in the captured soul of a Miguel Eltordo who had escaped from Hell some time ago. Now, we have got to get a file on this case Martin, so I suggest that you get together with this rookie and you get together some story, the truth would be nice, and you bring it to me next week. Am I making myself clear?"

"Yes Sir."

"And think about what you are doing next time. You risked her life and she saved your butt." Joshua walked over to his drinks cabinet and poured out three glasses. "Your resignation isn't accepted and I look forward to handing you two back over to Doug, who I also assume will withdraw his resignation."

"Doug!" Martin downed his drink. "I'd better go and tell Doug."

"Here." Joshua refilled his glass, "I wouldn't go just yet."

64

Jayne spread the sheet out around her and wondered if she was approaching this in the right way. Doug thought she had gone for ever so maybe coming back to his house to find her in his bed wasn't the best way to discover she was alright. Was it a little cheap? What if he came upstairs and thought she was someone else? She heard the door open downstairs, it was too late to change her plan now. There was a clatter in the kitchen, a couple of clicks as switches were thrown and then footsteps towards the stairs. Jayne's heart stuck in her throat. She was more nervous now than she had been when she had been sword fighting demons. The footsteps changed as they started up the staircase. She could just pretend that she was asleep, rather than trying to lie seductively under the sheets. Doug appeared at the top of the stairs, halfway through removing a jumper, and turned to face the wardrobe. He folded the jumper and reached up to put it away. He looked different in jeans and with no tie.

"Oh my God!" He stood with his back to the bed but he had caught sight of her in the mirror. "Tell me I am not dreaming."

"You are not dreaming."

"How?" He turned around, smiling. "I thought you were gone for good."

"So did I." She knelt up in front of him, wrapped in the sheet. He took her face between his hands and kissed her.

"Oh thank God you are back." He hugged her into his body. "What happened?"

"I'll tell you all about it." She pulled him down onto the bed, "after."

65

Thomas O'Malley had been in charge of new intakes at St Luke's seminary for nearly five years now and he thought he did it quite well. He thought he got on rather well with youths, it was one of the benefits of being cursed with the same name as a cartoon cat. But this was different; never in all his days had he seen an intake like this. You got the odd few that you couldn't really see as priests. They generally left and became religious education teachers. You got the odd one or two who had a slight problem with the vows but never anything like this. The boy had had such perfect references. He read like a saint on paper. His own priest had highly recommended him. Thomas pulled out the letter and dialled the number at the top of the page. He had to remove the ear plugs to check it was ringing. The music was still blaring. He had moved the boy down to the private chambers beside his office so that the other boys weren't disturbed. Since the move he had invested in ear plugs. The singer wailed and screamed out the lyrics.

"Six, six, six, the number of the beast." Thomas squashed the phone to his ear.

"Hello, is that Father Derek. It's Thomas O'Malley here from Saint Luke's seminary. I wonder if I could have a word. I think we have a slight problem with Richard. Young Richard Elliot."

Epilogue

The door swung open and Joshua and Doug took a step inside. In the distance sat a man at a desk. He looked up and seemed to positively jump from his seat, jogging down the office to meet them

"Jacque, it's great to see you again." He slid his hand past the outstretched palm and up to the forearm where he gripped it, his other hand seeking the elbow and pulling Doug in close. "Does this need to be a private audience?" He whispered in his ear. The use of his real name had made Doug tense a little.

"I'm not sure who I can trust." He replied. Their host turned to look at Joshua allowing his bright blue eyes to rest for far longer than was conventionally acceptable.

"I trust Joshua." Their host replied, released Doug's arm and led them back towards his desk and the chairs that had been set out for them.

"I hear you have been up to quite a lot since we last met." Michael ran his hands back through his bright blond hair and settled back in his chair. "What do you need to talk to me about?"

"Coincidences." Doug replied and lowered the package he had been carrying onto the floor beside his chair. It made a metallic clang as he did so and for a second all eyes focused on the cloth covered bundle.

"There is no such thing as a coincidence." Michael lent forward. "What has been happening?"

"When we last met I had just finished my rehab and was about to go back to work."

"Yes." Michael agreed in the sort of voice that made it clear they all knew about the circumstances leading up to that and it did not need to be discussed again.

"I think I have been followed most days since then." Doug sat back and crossed his legs at the ankles trying to convey a air of calmness that he did not possess.

"It's not all about you." Michael quipped with a slight smile across his lips. He turned to Joshua and raised a questioning eyebrow.

"I have not requested that he be followed." Joshua confirmed, as if he needed to.

"They aren't good, I lose them most days. A few weeks ago I lost them by ducking into the arrivals hall."

"A good place to lose people." Michael took a sip of the water that was sitting beside his paperwork.

"I wasted a few minutes by having a coffee with a new arrival." Doug prepared himself for what now seemed a ridiculous sequence of events. "The next day this new arrival appears at HQ for training." Michael shot him a glance from under his eyebrows.

"I thought the people we trained had been up here for years." He looked across at Joshua for confirmation.

"That's usually the case. You didn't mention she was a new arrival." This was news to Joshua.

"I thought the process had changed whilst I had been in rehab." Doug turned back to face Michael. "The next day Dickson tries to cut her from the training programme and I find myself being given her as a new recruit to train one on one."

Michael turned to Joshua again.

"That was me." Joshua admitted. "Doug said he saw something in her."

"I then decide to train her the way I used to train people. No books and notes, actual experience. So, I send her down to what should have been an empty safe house."

"I'm guessing is wasn't." Michael waved at a secretary who had just entered the room and three coffees appeared on the table.

"No, Martin was down there in the middle of the big Dali Lama case. He manages to remove any tagging system we invent." This was clearly a cause of frustration for Joshua.

"Now we have an untrained rookie down with Martin in the middle of one of the biggest cases that we have. No sooner has she got there than all of the transport systems go off line. She's stuck."

"This is beginning to look a little suspicious." Michael picked up his coffee and took a sip.

"Oh, it gets better." Doug continued, "Martin takes her out to meet one of his contacts and whilst they are out they discover that she is actually an angel." Michael stopped mid swallow.

"When was the last time we missed an angel at arrivals?"

"Decades ago." Joshua rested his foot up on his opposite knee. "I checked when this was first brought to light. They haven't missed an angel for over 26 years."

"Now we have a rookie, untrained, untagged angel stuck down on Earth in the middle of the Dali lama case. We find out the spectral warriors have been activated." Doug summarised where they were.

"Did either of you, at any point, think you should maybe have mentioned this to me?" Michael looked from one to the other and back again. "You're going to tell me it gets better, aren't you?"

"A lot." Doug took a mouthful of coffee.

"Continue." Michael waved him on.

"Martin decides that the best way to sort out the Dali lama issue is to send Jayne,"

"That's the name of the rookie." Joshua added helpfully but just got a stern glance from Michael.

"He sends Jayne back in time."

"He what?" Michael looked up slowly, his gaze resting on Doug. "It is forbidden for an angel to send people around in time."

"He didn't actually do it. He had help...from his contact."

Michael sat slowly back into his chair and pushed the fingertips of his hands together before bringing them up to his pursed lips.

"His contact is someone who can transport people through time without breaking the commandment that angels should not do this?" They all knew what he was asking, without actually spelling it out.

"Yes."

"You gave an untrained, untagged angel into the care of an agent from Hell?" Surely not, Michael thought, but he knew what answer was coming.

"Yes."

"Just to be perfectly clear, did you at any point think this was a good idea? And did you know about it?" Michael pointed to Joshua first.

"I did not know about it." he replied. Michael then pointed to Doug.

"I did not know about it either at the time and obviously did not think it was a good idea when I found out, although to be fair, it worked."

"I wish I could gloss over the fact that it worked. It was possibly a master piece of an idea but I must admit when I heard about what had happened the untrained untagged angel bit was missing from the story." He looked across at Doug again, "does it get better?"

"I'm afraid it does. Once they had stopped the demon possessing the Dali lama's body they discover that the only person who can move Jayne out of the time loop is the contact from Hell."

"Obviously." Michael added.

"So, he takes her back to his place in Hell, with the plan of getting her to the embassy so she can be returned to us."

"He doesn't sound like your average citizen of Hell." Michael finished his coffee and pushed the cup to the side.

"Only by now the spectral warriors have realised where the untagged angel is and it's going to be a fight to get across to the embassy. So, they have to arm themselves." Doug leant down to the side of the chair and lifted up the cloth package, laying it carefully on Michael's desk before flicking back the covers to reveal a sword.

"My sword!" Michael looked from the sword to Doug. His fingers reached out towards it and a faint flame licked along its blade. "That's been missing for centuries. Where was it?"

"It was under the contact's bed."

"Under his bed!" After a few hesitant touches, Michael picked up the hilt of the sword, stood up behind the table and swung it a few times around his head. Flames leapt along its blade and shot towards the ceiling. "I had the highest angels in the land scour Heaven and Earth for this and it was under his bed?"

"Jayne used it to fight her way across the square and get into the embassy." Doug offered an explanation as to how it had come back into their possession.

"Impressive!"

"Very." Doug pulled a phone out of his pocket. "I filmed this this morning." He pressed play on the screen and slid the phone across the desk to Michael. He stopped and looked at the video. He picked it up and stared at the screen. If colour could have faded from the brilliance of his face then it would have done so. He looked from the screen to Doug and back to the screen.

"I need to see this girl." He lowered the sword to his side, the flame extinguishing with a faint pop, and marched across the office towards the door. "Bring her to me."

Doug started after him. Joshua reached across to the phone and pressed the play button again. It was poorly lit but it was clear to see Jayne standing there, the sword on the table. As she reached to pick it up flames shot along its blade and caught the edge of the curtain sending flames up towards the ceiling. The angle of shooting went a bit crazy as the person holding the phone clearly tried to put out the fire.

"Oh, dear God." Joshua pocketed the phone and followed Doug out of the room.

Follow the further adventure of Doug, Jayne, Martin and Simon in "The Children of Michael" the second book in the Third Sphere novels.

Other books by Janet Philp

Burke Now and Then

'More thrilling than any who dunnit'. This retelling of the Burke and Hare story tells the grisly truth behind the supply of the bodies for the teaching of medicine in 1820's Edinburgh. A unique view point from the Earthly remains of William Burke, which hang in the Anatomical Museum of the University of Edinburgh. Acclaimed by the British Society of the history of medicine as 'refreshing' with 'the device of using Burke as narrator pays off handsomely to fashion a vivid description of the affair'. A must for anyone interested in the history of medicine.

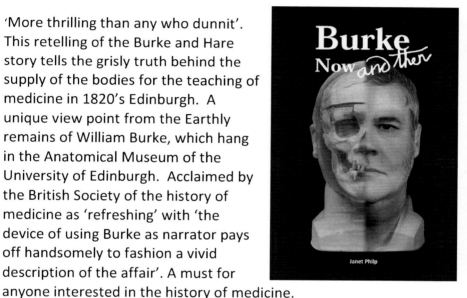

Available on Amazon as a paperback or e book

The Anatomy Pirates

The true story behind the skull
casts of a pirate crew that sit in
the Anatomical Museum of the
University of Edinburgh.
Treachery, poisoning and
murder.
The truth is far worse than any
Hollywood film.
Complete with the full court
proceedings, the story is laid
out for the readers enjoyment
as well as exploring the other
work that has been done with
the skull casts.

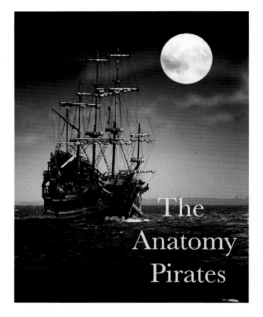

Available on Amazon as a paperback or e book

The Lance Grows Rusty

Returning from a research trip from Spain, Duncan Twort finds himself being deserted by best friends, cajoled into an ill-advised affair and in the middle of a deadly disease outbreak. Will be stay and face the music, or run away? A fictional tale of research scientists inspired by the author's ten years of experience in that field.

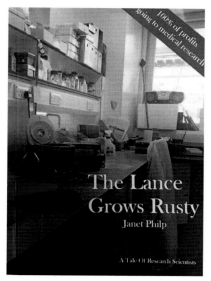

Available on Amazon as a paperback or e book